THE DEBT

INSTALLMENT TWO

THE DEBT

THE DEBT

TURN OFF THE LIGHTS

INSTALLMENT TWO

PHILLIP GWYNNE

Kane Miller
A DIVISION OF EDC PUBLISHING

First American Edition 2014
Kane Miller, A Division of EDC Publishing

Copyright © Phillip Gwynne 2013
Cover and internal design copyright © Allen & Unwin 2013
Cover and text design by Natalie Winter
Cover photography: (boy) by Alan Richardson Photography,
  model: Nicolai Laptev; (free running & jump) by Getty Images

For information contact:
Kane Miller, A Division of EDC Publishing
PO Box 470663
Tulsa, OK 74147-0663

www.kanemiller.com
www.edcpub.com
www.usbornebooksandmore.com

Library of Congress Control Number: 2013953411

Printed and bound in the United States of America
1 2 3 4 5 6 7 8 9 10
ISBN: 978-1-61067-304-4

To Goldie,
for your help

THE CICADA FEELING

Don't look, Dom, I told myself as I ran past Imogen's house.

But I couldn't help myself: I looked and she wasn't there and I had this cicada feeling. I call it that because sometimes around our house there are all these cicadas. Except they aren't really, because when you pick one up, it's empty, just a shell, and it collapses in your hand.

The cicada feeling.

When I reached the main entrance to Halcyon Grove, Samsoni, the security guard, said, "You're better off running inside, Mr. Silvagni," which is what he always says.

I was about to say what I always say – "No topographical variation inside, Samsoni" – but I hesitated.

Maybe Samsoni was right, maybe I was better off running inside today, lap after lap of the perimeter of Halcyon Grove.

Outside, bad stuff happened. Outside, white vans came up from behind and you lost four minutes of your life.

Outside rednecks shot at you.

Outside …

"No topographical variation inside, eh, Mr. Silvagni?" said Samsoni.

"No, there isn't," I said, and continued running.

A few minutes later, I heard footsteps behind me.

Who in the blazes is that? I took a quick look over my shoulder, my pulse quickening.

It was a balding man in a bulging tracksuit. Despite all his huffing and puffing, he certainly didn't look like any Big Bad Wolf. I slowed down, however, and let him shuffle past. Usually I wouldn't let this happen. I'd shift up a gear and show him the bottom of my Asics. But The Debt had made me paranoid, so paranoid that I let Chrome Dome have his moment of middle-age glory. And I imagined him at work, later in the day, bragging to his colleagues. "There's this kid, right, thinks he's pretty hot, but I sure showed him a thing or two."

I finished my run, but instead of going over to Gus's house for breakfast I went straight back to my bedroom.

As usual, the ClamTop was sitting on my desk. As usual, it was shut, clammed tight.

One of the cardinal rules of The Debt is that absolutely nobody is allowed to help you. But surely Dad could answer general questions, I thought. Like how long between installments.

I found him on the treadmill doing his workout, watching one of those morning shows on the plasma. A spokesperson from Earth Hour was talking about their upcoming event.

"A lot of businesses here on the Gold Coast are behind us," she said. "And we urge your viewers to turn off their lights as well. Remember, it's only for an hour."

"That date again?" asked the interviewer.

"Saturday the twenty-fifth of March," said the woman.

"Maybe even the residents of Halcyon Grove could find the off switch this year," said the interviewer, chuckling, enjoying his own joke.

He held up an aerial photo, taken during last Earth Hour, of Halcyon Grove with lights blazing; it looked like something from *Star Wars*, a spaceship hurtling through deep, dark space.

I turned my attention back to Dad. He really had a terrible running style: shoulders hunched, body leaning forward, an excessively pronated gait.

It's not as if I was going to tell him that, though. And it's not as if the treadmill was either.

All it did was offer encouragement, in this annoying California voice. "Congratulations! You have reached your first programmed goal! Keep up the good work! Champ!"

"Hi, Dad," I said. "How's it going?"

"Great to see you, buddy boy," he said.

When my dad said, "Great to see you, buddy boy," you knew they weren't just words tumbling out of his mouth, you knew he really meant it.

"Can I ask you a question about The Debt?"

Immediately, Dad stopped running. The treadmill wasn't happy.

"Great run! But you haven't reached your second programmed goal! Champ!"

A look of irritation appeared on Dad's sweat-sheened face.

"You know I can't –" he started, before I cut him off by saying, "It's just a general question."

The look of annoyance was replaced by a forced smile.

"Of course, son."

"How long did you have to wait between installments?"

Dad dabbed at the sweat on his brow with a small white towel.

"A couple of weeks," he said. "Pretty sure it was a couple of weeks."

Dad stepped off the treadmill, and the treadmill responded by saying, "Great workout! Hope to see you again soon!"

"I know this Debt thing has thrown you a bit, and I can't blame you," said Dad, throwing an arm around my shoulder. "I was pretty much the same when it happened to me. But do you know what? The Debt is not necessarily an imposition. What I mean to say is, it's not necessarily a burden. In some ways, it's an opportunity. Turn adversity into advantage."

Right, so it was an advantage to be forced to pay off a debt that your great-great-great-great-grandfather incurred?

It was an advantage to live under the constant threat of amputation?

Especially for a runner like me.

"Like Gus?" I said, thinking of his stump and prosthetic leg.

"Dom, I know you love your grandfather," said Dad, and then something else came into his voice, a kind of steel, and he said, "but it was me who dragged the family out of the gutter, not him. You got that? And it's your job to keep us out of it."

A look came over his face, like he was recollecting something from long ago.

"My hands are bloody but unbowed," he said, his voice sounding uncharacteristically fragile.

But then he seemed to pull himself together.

Checking his watch, he said, "Better get a move on, Tokyo Stock Exchange just opened."

HOSPITAL

All day at school Dad's words kept echoing in my head: "my hands are bloody but unbowed."

But were they his words? It just didn't sound like something he'd say.

So I did exactly what teachers do when they think a student has plagiarized something: I googled the suspect phrase. And all that came up was this poem *Invictus* which included the line: *my head is bloody, but unbowed.*

I figured that maybe he'd done it at school or something and he'd remembered it incorrectly.

No big deal.

Besides, I had other stuff to think about, like how to get to the coin shop after school.

It proved to be really straightforward: after one bus and a bit of walking, I was standing outside

Coast Coins and Stamps: Your One Stop Shop For All Your Numismatic & Philatelic Needs.

I guess I'd been expecting someplace bigger, more modern looking, something that was like its website, but the shop itself was somewhat small and somewhat shabby.

I could feel the coin's weight in my pocket, the coin Otto Zolton-Bander aka the Zolt aka the Facebook Bandit had dropped in our swimming pool from a light plane.

Of course, I'd researched it on the net. No matter where I started: Google, Wikipedia, various coin websites, I always ended up at the same place: the coin was a 1933 Ultra High Relief Saint-Gaudens Double Eagle.

According to Wikipedia, there were 445,500 of these $20 coins minted, but they were never circulated and were all melted down by the US Treasury.

All except for two official specimens and an unknown number that were stolen from the US Mint.

So far twenty of those stolen coins had been discovered and in 2002 one was sold at auction for US$7.59 million. Yes, that's right: US$7.59 million!

Was I walking around with US$7.59 million in my pocket?

I was pretty sure the coin wasn't real, however. Because according to my research there were a lot of replica 1933 Ultra High Relief Saint-Gaudens Double Eagles around. And this had to be one of them.

Didn't it?

Except I couldn't find anything on the coin that said it was a replica.

According to Wikipedia, some of these replicas had *copy* stamped across the eagle's abdomen, or some sort of seal under the US motto on the reverse. My coin, however, had neither of these.

Which was the reason I was standing outside the somewhat small, somewhat shabby Coast Coins and Stamps while two debate teams were going at it in my head.

But what it if is the real thing? said one team. *Won't Dom get arrested or something?*

But it can't be the real thing, said the other team. *Do you really think a fifteen-year-old kid is walking around with US$7.59 million in his pocket?*

In the end both teams figured the best thing to do was just go inside and ask.

Especially since, according to Coast Coins and Stamps website, their "absolute discretion" was assured.

As soon as I entered the shop I had "somewhat dusty" to add to "somewhat small" and "somewhat shabby."

So "somewhat dusty" that I sneezed several times.

"Gesundheit," said the woman behind the counter, looking up from the book she was reading.

The title, I noticed, was *Great Shipwrecks of the World* by E. Lee Marx. I recognized the name because last week I'd seen a program on the Discovery Channel all about him, the world's greatest treasure hunter.

I'm not sure why, but I wasn't expecting a woman.

Especially not one like this, dressed in velvet, swathed in scarves, eyes ringed with kohl, a crucifix with a very crucified-looking Jesus hanging around her neck. She looked like the fortune-teller who set up her stall at the psychic fair that took place every month at the Chevron Heights shopping center.

"Thanks," I said.

"How can I help you?" she said, putting the book on the counter.

"Um," I said. Followed by another "um" and yet another "um."

All the time the woman smiled encouragingly at me with her fortune-teller's face.

Eventually it worked because I was able to coax something apart from "um" out of my mouth.

"I have this coin," I blurted.

"Coins are my absolute passion, so you've come to the right place," she said.

"I'm pretty sure it's a fake," I said, my hand in my pocket feeling the coin, its smoothness, the weight of it.

"Well, if it is I'll soon let you know," she said.

"Here it is," I said, putting the coin on the counter.

She didn't even bother to pick it up before she said, "Yes, that's a fakeroony, alright."

"You can tell already?"

"Yep. There are quite a few Double Eagles coming out of China, Korea. Some very nice ones too. But that isn't one."

Okay, it was exactly what I expected, but I couldn't help but feel gutted.

The woman continued. "There's the eagle's eye for a start – it shouldn't be black like that."

"It shouldn't?" I said, and now I was actually feeling a bit ashamed of my fakeroony Double Eagle.

"I'm sorry to bother you," I said, scooping up the coin and putting it back into my pocket.

"No bother at all!" she said. "Great to see a young person with numismatic interests. If you find something else I'd love to see it."

She handed me her business card. Her name was Eve Carides, Numismatist.

I thanked Eve Carides, Numismatist, and left.

My phone rang. *Zoe calling …*

It was actually a bit of a shock to see her name,

because I hadn't heard from Zoe since the Zolt and I had left her at the airport on Reverie Island.

And immediately I wondered if her call had something to do with the Double Eagle, the coin her brother had dropped in my pool.

"Zoe!" I answered.

"Where are you?" she said.

"I'm on my way to Mater Hospital," I said.

The line dropped out.

I called her back but she didn't answer.

Weird, I thought. But then again, Zoe was weird.

Fortunately I was able to catch a bus at a nearby stop that took me directly to Mater Hospital.

Through the front doors, third floor, turn right, turn left, turn left again, past the nurses' station where Siobhan, the really nice Irish nurse, was writing something on a chart.

"Here he is now, our favorite visitor," she said, smiling up at me.

"Any change?" I said.

She shook her head.

I continued on, and knocked softly on the door.

"Come in," came Mrs. Jazy's voice.

I went in, and Imogen was sitting there, next to Tristan, her hand on his hand.

Imogen who hadn't talked to me since Tristan's accident. Imogen who hadn't replied to one of my texts or one of my emails. Imogen who no longer stood at the window and waved at me when I went past her house on my morning run. That Imogen.

"Hi, Imogen," I said, thinking that she would have to say something to me now.

But I was wrong, because all she did was look away and turn her attention back to Tristan. I didn't know whether Mrs. Jazy knew exactly what was going on, but she threw me a sympathetic look nonetheless.

"Siobhan said no change," I said to her.

"The specialist this morning was very happy," said Mrs. Jazy.

I sat on the opposite side of the bed to Imogen, reached out and put my hand over Tristan's other hand. It felt cold. Dead. But all the machines that were connected to him were making lots of reassuring noises, the monitors displaying reassuring numbers.

"I better get going," said Imogen, getting up.

"Thanks so much for coming," said Mrs. Jazy.

"See you around," I said as Imogen walked past me.

She glanced at me, our eyes met, and for the briefest of moments it seemed like she was going to say something. No such luck. She continued on out the door.

Five minutes later the door opened and Mr. Jazy appeared, carrying flowers and containers of what smelled like Thai takeout. His beard, once so abundant, like old-growth forest, now looked thin, over-logged. And his eyes seemed to have sunk right back into his head.

"Those inept police finally found my Merc at the Reverie airport," he said. "Apparently it was used by that young man Zolton-Bander."

Here we go again. Feign complete surprise, Dom.

I feigned complete surprise.

"Really," I said. "Is the car okay?"

Once upon a time, and not so long ago, I didn't have to do this stuff: feign complete surprise, tell endless lies. But now, ever since The Debt, it seemed like that's all I did. It seemed as if my whole life was driven by it.

"There was some minor damage," he said. "But the police have impounded it for forensic testing."

Forensic testing!

Of course, they'd find pieces of me in the car: hair, skin particles, whatever, and then my DNA would end up in a central database somewhere.

And if I'm ever DNA-tested in the future and they run a database match they'll find out I was there!

"Are you okay, Dom?" asked Mrs. Jazy.

"Can you please text me if there's any change?" I said, getting up.

"Of course I can," she said.

Mrs. Jazy stood up and it was hug time.

I knew I couldn't deny her one, not with her son comatose in the bed, but it really was pretty excruciating.

I mean, it wasn't my fault that Tristan was like he was: I didn't make him steal that Maserati, I didn't make him drive it like a madman. No, it wasn't my fault, but if we hadn't gone to the Zolt's lair, if we hadn't been shot at by Red Bandana, then I didn't think Tristan would be in a coma right now. So it wasn't my fault but it was my fault. When Mrs. Jazy had finished her hug, I said good-bye to both of them and hurried out of the door.

ZOE AGAIN

There was a doctor in the corridor, stethoscope around her neck, clipboard in her hand, all the usual doctor accessories.

No surprise in encountering a doctor in the corridor, it was a hospital after all, but what was surprising was the size of this particular doctor.

She was a very small doctor, a pocket-doc.

She was also, I noticed, a very young doctor.

She must've graduated from high school at the age of three.

"Zoe!" I said, remembering the last time I'd seen her, that tragic look on her face as her brother and I were just about to get on a plane.

A plane that didn't have tray tables, in-flight entertainment, or even a real pilot for that matter.

"Shhh!" she said, straightening her glasses.

"Let's walk."

"Is that ludicrous disguise really necessary?" I said as I followed her down the corridor.

She looked at me as if I'd just asked her if breathing, or having a mobile phone, was necessary. *Of course it's necessary, you imbecile.*

Although Zoe had this awkward sort of splay-footed gait, she actually got along at a fair clip and I had to throw in a few skips to keep up.

"Where we going?" I said.

"Somewhere very public."

That somewhere very public ended up being Emergency.

Okay, I knew that the Gold Coast was a pretty violent sort of place – the newspapers had been calling it the Murder Capital of Australia – but I didn't realize it was this violent.

Seriously, Emergency looked like the aftermath of a terrorist bomb.

There were broken arms, broken legs, broken noses, broken heads; there were blood-soaked bandages; there were babies screaming; and to top it off, a skeletal man dressed in an overcoat was rocking back and forth, saying over and over again, "It hurts, it hurts, it hurts so much."

"Perfection," said Zoe. "Purr-fection."

She pointed to two empty seats in the far corner.

"Let's sit there."

Once we were seated I took a closer look at Zoe.

Her glasses seemed even more lopsided than usual and she had what looked like sand in her hair. The ludicrous disguise, the lopsided glasses: it was difficult to take Zoe seriously, but I knew that it would be a mistake not to.

A woman in a headscarf, a bundled baby in her arms, approached.

"Please help me, doctor," she said. "Baby very sick, doctor."

"What are the child's symptoms?" said Zoe, hand going to stethoscope.

"She's not really a doctor," I said, removing the stethoscope from around Zoe's neck. "She's got, you know, serious mental issues."

The woman still didn't look convinced, so I nudged Zoe.

"He's right," she said to the woman. "Not quite right in the head."

Reluctantly, the woman took her sick baby back to her seat.

"So what is it?" I said to Zoe, though I pretty much knew what the answer would be.

She didn't let me down. "It's Otto."

"I don't think he died in that plane crash," I said gently, worried that she might think her brother was dead.

"Of course he didn't die in that stupid plane crash," she said.

The man in the overcoat had ceased his lament, the babies had stopped crying and, suddenly, it was eerily quiet in Emergency.

"So obviously he's contacted you?" I said.

Zoe ignored my question, something she did with frustrating regularity.

"Did my brother ever give you anything?" she asked.

"What sort of thing?" I said.

Zoe gave me this do-we-have-to-play-these-stupid-games? look before she said, "A coin sort of thing."

"So he wants it back?" I said, my hand automatically going into my pocket.

"You still have it?" she said, and she seemed genuinely surprised.

"Well, it's not as if it's got any market value," I said.

There was a ruckus at the reception desk.

A couple of scruffy street kids were arguing with the triage nurse.

"I need to see a doctor now!" a boy screamed.

Even from where I was sitting I could see his spittle flying.

He did look pretty sick, though – very skinny and very pale.

A girl gently pushed the boy away and leaned in closer to the nurse. I couldn't hear what she was saying, but I could tell that her tone was much more reasonable than her friend's. A doctor appeared, and the kids disappeared with him behind a door.

"I wouldn't be so sure that it doesn't have any market value," said Zoe.

"What's that supposed to mean?" I said.

Zoe didn't answer my question but suddenly seemed very interested in her fingernails instead. As far as fingernails went, especially girl fingernails, they were pretty wrecked: chipped and chewed.

Eventually she looked away from her cuticles and at me and said, "Okay, I'm not sure why I trust you, but I do."

I smiled at her – hey, I'm a pretty trustworthy sort of guy.

She adjusted her glasses and said, enunciating very clearly, "Maybe the coin is not what it seems."

What did she mean by that? Was it hollow? Did it have something inside?

"So basically you want it back?" I said.

Zoe had to think about this for a while.

But then she said, again using that enunciated delivery, "Where exactly is the coin?"

She trusted me, or so she said. But did I trust her?

I wasn't sure.

But my hand obviously did, because it brought out the fake Double Eagle from my pocket.

"You carry it around with you?" she said.

"It's a fake," I said. "Why not?"

I didn't want to tell her that it had become a sort of charm for me, that its weight in my pocket felt oddly comforting.

"Where're you going after here?" she said.

"Home," I said.

"So you're, what, catching a bus or something?"

She sure was behaving weirdly, even for somebody whose default behavior setting was weird.

"Yes, I'm catching a bus or something," I said.

"I'm out of here," said Zoe, getting up.

And then she was gone.

Just like that – there one minute, all weird and Zoe-ish, gone the next.

The skeletal man in the overcoat started up again. "It hurts, it hurts, it hurts so much."

I figured it was time for me to get going too.

HINTERLAND

In the end I decided to walk home. As I reached Chevron Heights, next to the Coast Home Loans office, my phone rang.

Zoe calling ... it said, and to tell the truth, I was kind of annoyed.

What was she, some sort of stalker?

But there again, Zoe wasn't a call-for-nothing sort of chick. Actually she was more of a call-to-stick-some-spyware-on-your-phone sort of chick.

So I answered. "Hi, Zoe."

But there was no reply, just a lot of muffled sounds, the sort you get when somebody accidently calls you when their phone is in their pocket or at the bottom of their schoolbag.

And that's exactly what I'd assumed had happened until I heard Zoe's muffled voice say, "So where are you taking me?"

"None of your business," said a gruff male voice.

I realized then what was happening: Zoe's paranoia had been justified, after all – she'd been kidnapped, and she'd managed to hit redial on her phone, to alert me.

"It is my business!" said Zoe.

"Gag her," said the voice, and then there was a *thump!* and Zoe screamed.

"Are you okay, Zoe?" I yelled, before I realized that wasn't the smartest move.

If they found out what she'd done, that she'd alerted somebody, there might be even more *thump!* sounds.

So I kept my mouth closed.

There was more scuffling, but then Zoe said two things: the first sounded like "iCloud" and the second sounded like "yamashita."

Okay, you don't get much more random than that. I figured the *thump!* had already done something really bad to her brain.

The muffled noises continued, but the gagged Zoe was understandably quiet after that.

And I didn't have a clue what to do.

The cops, I thought. *Debt or no Debt, now's the time to get the cops involved.*

I dialed triple zero, and was listening to the phone ring on the other end when I came to my senses: there was no way I could get the cops involved.

Somebody answered just as I hit end.

I had to sort out this mess myself.

But how?

Then it occurred to me: Zoe Zolton-Bander was not a random sort of chick, even a Zoe Zolton-Bander who'd just been thumped.

I knew what iCloud was, but what did it have to do with Zoe being kidnapped?

I took out my phone, got on to the net.

It didn't take me long to find it: iCloud had a service called Find My iPhone.

I downloaded the app onto my iPhone and opened it.

It wanted an email.

I logged on to Mozilla, found Zoe's email and entered that. Now it wanted a password. I entered *yamashita*, the second thing Zoe had said.

It worked! I was logged on to Zoe's iCloud account.

And under the heading "List Of Configured Devices" was "Zoe's iPhone."

I double-clicked on this and a map appeared.

Zoe and her phone were just turning off the Pacific Highway and onto the road to Tallebudgera Valley.

Now all I had to do was follow her.

I put out my hand to catch a cab and then realized that probably wasn't going to work.

Only in movies do people hop into cabs and say, "Follow that car!"

A scooter, with a pizza delivery boy aboard, pulled into the parking lot of Big Pete's.

I watched as he got off and hurried inside.

You're not seriously considering ...? I asked myself.

Obviously I was, however, because I was already running across the road, dodging the oncoming traffic.

Just as I'd hoped, the pizza delivery boy had left his helmet on the seat and the keys in the ignition.

I'd ridden a motorbike before, last year when we'd gone to Bali for vacation, but that had only been up and down a bumpy road a couple of times.

What choice did I have, though?

I put on the helmet, got on board and started the ignition.

"Hey, you!"

It was him, the delivery boy, now laden with pizza boxes.

I twisted the throttle and the scooter wobbled off and into the traffic.

In Bali I'd seen much younger kids than me riding motorbikes. Often with a couple more kids on the back.

This was Australia, not Bali, and I was a fifteen year old riding a scooter on one of the busiest roads on the Coast. This time it felt like everybody, and I mean everybody, was checking me out.

I glanced at my iPhone.

They were still on the road to Tallebudgera Valley, heading into the hinterland, so I figured I had to turn left at the next intersection.

But just as I got there the lights turned red and I had no choice but to stop.

I kept my head low, I tucked my elbows in; I wanted to look as small, and anonymous, as possible.

Nobody said anything to me, and when the lights turned green I was able to keep going.

As I headed east, the traffic thinned out.

Eventually the houses gave way to undulating hills.

Now that it was getting dark, now that the traffic was thinner, I was starting to feel less vulnerable.

Again, I took out my iPhone, checked the app.

Zoe and her captors were heading deeper into the Tallebudgera Valley.

The air suddenly became cooler as the road reared up into the range.

The scooter's 80 cc of internal combustion engine wasn't happy with the work it had to do and started making a high-pitched whining sound.

Still, we were getting there.

And when I checked Find My iPhone again and saw that they'd stopped I felt even better – maybe I wouldn't be chasing them all the way to Alice Springs, after all.

Tallebudgera Valley 7 km said a sign, and then just beyond it there was another one, *We're Adding New Lanes, Expect Significant Delays.*

Nobody was working this late, however, and all the heavy machinery was just sitting there.

"Not far now," I told the scooter, and it was right then that I noticed the fuel was on empty.

It's okay, I assured myself. *The big old warning light hasn't come on yet.*

Three seconds later the engine spluttered and we came to a stop: the fuel had run out.

I now had another fact to add to my collection: many scooters do not have big old fuel warning lights.

I pushed the scooter off the road, hid it behind a bulldozer, and considered my options.

This didn't take long because there weren't many. I could walk or I could try to hitch a lift.

If I went by foot it would take me at least two hours to reach Zoe, and by that time …

Hitching a lift would be quicker, of course. But there were very few cars on the road, and people are reluctant enough to give strangers a lift during the day, let alone in the dark.

Again I checked Find My iPhone – they still hadn't moved.

"Shiitake mushroom!" I said, kicking the bulldozer hard in the tire.

Not that it was its fault, but I had to kick something and it was the most convenient something.

I gave another "Shiitake mushroom!" and the bulldozer another undeserving kick.

Again I had that thought: *It's time to get the cops involved in this.*

So I called triple-0.

Before I could say anything the woman on the other end said, "You called triple-0 earlier?"

"Not really, I hung up," I said. "But you really need to listen, my friend has been kidnapped –'

But that was as far as I got, because the woman said, "Prank-calling triple-0 is a very serious offense, young man."

"I'm not prank-calling …" I started, but then I realized I was getting nowhere and I hung up. Again.

The bulldozer copped another hefty kick in the tire.

Again I checked Find My iPhone.

They were in the same place.

I had to do something.

I had to find a way to get there.

I was just about to walk over to the road, stick my thumb out, when I had a thought.

Okay, it was a pretty outrageous thought, but that was something The Debt had taught me: all thoughts, not matter how outrageous, are worth considering.

I'd seen how the Zolt had hot-wired Mr. Jazy's Mercedes, seen how he'd yanked the wires out, seen how he'd stripped the wires, seen how he'd touched the wires together.

Surely a bulldozer couldn't be that much different.

I clambered up into the unlocked cabin.

Felt under the dashboard where the ignition was.

There was a tangle of wires.

Yeah, right!

Otto Zolton-Bander had been stealing cars since he was a little kid. Of course he was going to be an expert at it.

Okay, I'd just stolen a motorbike but apart from that I'd hardly stolen anything in my whole life, let alone a car, let alone a bulldozer.

Of course I'd be useless at it.

I let go of the wires and collapsed back into the seat.

What a useless childhood I'd had! Privileged but underprivileged.

I took out my iPhone.

Okay, I wasn't an expert, but I knew somebody who was.

I typed *how to hot-wire a bulldozer* into Google.

And got gold.

It turned out that bulldozers are diesel – you don't hot-wire them the same way you hot-wire a car. What you have to do is short the two terminals on the solenoid, this thing that's attached to the starter motor. It even gave a picture of a solenoid so I'd know what to look for.

God bless Google, I thought as I got down from the cabin.

I switched on the flashlight app, played the beam on the motor.

And there it was. It didn't look exactly like the one in the photo, but it looked enough like it for me to recognize it.

Now all I needed was something metal.

It didn't take long to find that either. On the side of the bulldozer there was a toolbox, and in there was a tire lever.

I touched one end of the tire lever onto one of the terminals and slowly brought the lever down until metal touched the other terminal.

Sparks flew, the starter motor whirred, the engine coughed a couple of times, and then it was away.

I clambered back into the cabin.

There was no steering wheel, just a joystick.

But it hadn't been that long since I'd seen the Zolt use one like this.

So I pushed it forward in the direction I wanted to go, twisted the throttle, and the bulldozer responded.

After a while, with the bulldozer rollicking along and my confidence growing, I turned the throttle to full and the speedometer needle crept past fifty kilometers per hour.

Weirdly enough, I felt much less conspicuous driving this vehicle, which was about as conspicuous as you could get, than I did on the scooter.

Because I knew that high up in the cabin, on the dark unfinished road, nobody could see me.

And if anybody in the cars that passed thought it was strange to see a bulldozer tooling along at this time of night, they didn't give any indication of this.

I spent some time familiarizing myself with the other controls, especially the lever that lowered the blade.

It occurred to me that not only had I gotten myself a pretty good set of wheels, I also had a pretty handy weapon. If anybody gave me a hard time, I could just lower the blade and bulldoze the living daylights out of them.

According to my iPhone they were only one kilometer away now, but they were to my left, not on this road.

I kept expecting there to be a crossroads, somewhere I could turn left, but there wasn't.

The road continued, its straightness a credit to its makers.

So despite the lack of road, I swung left anyway.

It was thin scrub and the bulldozer had no trouble plowing through it.

And when I reached a fence, I kept going. There was no time to find a gate.

The wire stretched tighter and tighter, making an eerie twanging sound before it snapped.

Half a kay to go, and up ahead I could make out the shape of a house, an old Queenslander up on stilts with an inside light on.

And next to it, a car.

I killed the ignition.

And felt a cold, prickly chill run through my body.

These weren't your everyday crims I was dealing with.

This was, in all possibility, The Debt.

If they cut off your leg when you were working for them, as they had done to my grandfather, what would they do if they found you working against them?

Okay, the answer to that was pretty easy: they would kill you.

Kill you slowly.

Kill you horribly.

Kill you piece by painful piece.

I climbed down from the cabin and made my way towards the house.

Without my bulldozer, without my weapon, I felt conspicuous again. And vulnerable. Boy, did I feel vulnerable.

As I got closer I could hear voices.

And, now, as well as a sense of dread, I felt an enormous sense of anticipation: at last I would know what they, The Debt, looked like.

I would know who they were.

Closer, and I could make out what the voices were saying.

"Just tell us where your brother's at, that's all we want to know," said a voice I immediately recognized.

I felt both tremendous relief and tremendous disappointment. It wasn't The Debt. Zoe had been kidnapped by her own uncle!

"Let me just slap the brat," said another voice.

"No!" said Zoe's uncle.

"Just a little tap and she'll be singing like Kylie."

I'd heard enough.

I hurried back to the bulldozer. Starting it up, I pushed the joystick forward, giving it plenty of throttle.

And I pointed it towards the house.

As I came closer, more lights came on.

People were outside.

People were yelling.

But by that time I'd reached the parked car.

It was Zoe's uncle's beloved – by him, anyway – Monaro.

The last time I'd see it, it had looked more like something you'd use to strain spaghetti, but he'd obviously spent time, effort and lots of putty on it since, because it was looking whole and shiny again.

"Let her go or I'll flatten your car," I yelled from up in the cabin.

"If I do, you promise not to touch me wheels?" said Zoe's uncle.

"I promise," I said.

And it didn't take much more than that, because suddenly Zoe was climbing up to join me in the cabin.

I pulled the joystick back and the bulldozer started reversing away from the car.

But suddenly Zoe leaned over and, with two hands, rammed the joystick forward.

"I promised to leave his car alone!" I said.

"I didn't," said Zoe. "Stupid amateurs could've spoiled everything!"

Spoiled what? I thought, but then there were horrible scraping sounds, and then horrible crunching sounds, but mixed up with that were also less horrible sounds, like the quite tuneful tinkling of glass shattering.

"Okay, I reckon that's enough," I said and pulled the joystick the other way.

I knew there would be damage, but I hadn't realized how much damage. Because Zoe's uncle's car really didn't look like a car anymore.

Once three-dimensional, it now appeared to have only two.

As we drove off, all I could hear was Zoe's uncle saying, in a voice not unlike the it-hurts man at the hospital, "Me car, what have they done to me car?"

As we made our way back, Zoe told me what had happened.

How she'd been kidnapped by her uncle and the Mattners.

"The Mattners!" I said, remembering that it was one of these Mattners who had turned the Monaro into a colander. "I thought they were your uncle's enemies."

"Nothing like the thought of money to bring enemies together," said Zoe.

"What money?" I said, but Zoe didn't answer and by this time we'd arrived back at the place where I'd taken the bulldozer.

I killed the motor.

"That how you got here?" said Zoe, pointing to the Big Pete's scooter. "Tasty."

"It ran out of fuel," I said.

"Then why didn't you put some more in?"

"Very funny," I said, but then I saw exactly what she was seeing: a forty-four-gallon drum clearly labeled *Gasoline*.

"Okay, but how do you get it out?" I said.

"Leave that to me," said Zoe. "On Reverie, we're always using OP gas."

"OP?"

"Other people's."

I watched as she found a piece of hose, as she opened the drum, as she used the hose to expertly siphon gasoline into the scooter's tank.

Thanks to OP gas, we were soon back on the road, me driving, Zoe on the back, heading down the range towards the Coast.

When we pulled up at the first set of red lights I noticed a black BMW just behind us.

At the next set of red lights it was still there.

"Do you reckon that BMW's tailing us?" I said to Zoe.

"What BMW?" she said.

Is she blind or something?

When we came to the next set of lights, the BMW was still on our tail. I braked suddenly and turned sharp left.

"Are they're still behind us?" I asked Zoe.

"I'm not sure," she said.

A quick look behind revealed that, indeed, they were still behind us.

Think, Dom!

Okay, they were faster than us, more powerful than us.

But they were also much bigger than us.

"Hold on!" I said.

There was a KFC up ahead.

I veered off the road, bounced over the gutter and onto the footpath.

The BMW slowed down so that it was traveling at the same speed as us.

I braked, turned into the drive-through. There was a car ahead of me, the driver leaning out of the window, talking into the speaker.

A screech behind: the BMW had also pulled into the drive-through.

I beeped my horn, and the driver of the car in front had just enough time to pull his head back in as we came flying through on the inside.

Another car in front, the girl at the counter was handing the driver her bag of chicken, her super-sized drink.

Again I beeped, but this time the driver wasn't so quick.

We flew through on the inside, collecting the chicken and the drink.

Lemonade poured into my helmet and the chicken disintegrated into a mess of secret herbs and spices.

We'd made it, though, and when I turned down a dark suburban street and then another one and then another one and pulled into an unlit park, I was pretty sure I'd lost them.

"Nice work," said Zoe, but there was a strange tone to her voice, almost as if she was disappointed.

"So where are you staying?" I asked.

"With friends," said Zoe.

"Which friends?" I said.

"Just friends, okay?" she said.

I remembered the sand in her hair.

"You slept on the beach last night, didn't you?" I said.

Zoe said nothing and I knew I was right.

Lots of people slept on the beach on the Gold Coast, and you never really heard of anything bad happening to them, but somehow I felt responsible for Zoe. I had to find her somewhere safer, somewhere less sandy, to sleep. My place? Not an option. But where? And then it came to me.

"You can stay at my grandfather's house," I said. "He'll be totally cool with that."

Zoe agreed, so I followed another series of backstreets until we reached a park close to Halcyon Grove. I cut the engine and wheeled the scooter behind some bushes. As we walked quickly to the main gate, I began to feel vulnerable again. What if they, whoever they were in the BMW, knew where I lived?

They could just wait for us, pick us off.

So it was a huge relief to see the stocky figure of Samsoni, to see those high walls, to see all that CCTV.

"She's with me," I said to Samsoni, attempting to usher Zoe straight through.

"I'm sorry, sir," he said, "but we still need to get her to sign in."

The last thing I wanted was for Zoe to sign in anywhere, and I thought about pulling rank on Samsoni.

"Do you know who my father is?" That sort of rank.

But I couldn't do that to him.

"Okay, you better sign in," I said to Zoe.

So Zoe signed in.

Samsoni looked at what she'd written and said, "And could I possibly see some ID, Ms. Huntington-Smyth?"

Ms. Huntington-Smyth! What was Zoe thinking?

She looked about as unHuntington as a Smyth could get.

Now I really would have to do the snotty-nosed-rich-kid thing and pull rank.

But before I could say anything, Samsoni had checked Zoe's ID and was saying, "Very good, Ms. Huntington-Smyth. Hope you enjoy your time in Halcyon Grove."

Zoe smiled at me as we continued walking.

Why had I been worried? Of course somebody as paranoid as Zoe would have phony ID. She probably had a whole polo team of phony IDs.

"Wow," said Zoe, looking around. "Is that, like, just one person's house?"

The house she had indicated actually was one person's house – cranky old Mr. Forehan's – but I wasn't going to let her know this.

"No," I lied. "A whole family lives in that one. You know, a whole extended family – grandparents, everything. Even got chickens out the back."

We continued past Imogen's house where all the lights were off. Past our house.

Zoe, please don't say anything. Please don't.

And she didn't, but I thought how crazy my response was. Zoe lived in something with wheels, and here I was embarrassed about my place.

"That's where I live," I said, pointing.

"Wow!" said Zoe. "It's like something out of a movie."

"And this is where my grandfather lives," I said.

We continued up the driveway.

"Gus, you there?" I called, pushing open the door.

There was no answer.

That was weird. Gus was always home at this time.

"Gus?" I called again.

Still no answer.

"Come on," I said to Zoe.

I didn't want her standing outside where anybody could see her.

"Gus?" I called for the third time, and this time there were footsteps.

"Where you been?" I said.

But it wasn't Gus who appeared in the corridor.

It was a man with a balaclava covering his face. A man with a baseball bat in his hands. And then another man. Also with a balaclava. Also with a baseball bat.

"Hand it over!" the man said to me.

"Hand what over?" I said.

"Hand it over now or your girlfriend gets her head knocked off," said the man.

"She's not my girlfriend …" I started, before Zoe cut me off, saying, "Just give him the Double Eagle."

I handed him the Double Eagle.

"Now on the floor, both of you," said the man.

I didn't need any further prompting – I hit the floor.

I waited until I heard them leave and a car start before I got up.

"You okay?" I asked Zoe.

But she was smiling this strange satisfied smile.

"I'm great," she said.

I didn't get it, and I must've had an I-don't-get-it look on my face, because Zoe said, "It's you, Dom. I don't know why, but stuff always happens when you're around. It's like you're bugged or something."

I still didn't get it.

"Mate," she said. "Somebody owns you."

Not long ago, it was Miranda telling me how "owned" I was. Now Zoe was doing the same. It was really starting to rankle.

Nobody owns me!

"So you totally set me up?" I said, thinking of all the risks I'd taken to save Zoe from her uncle and the Mattners. "After all I did for you."

Zoe shrugged and said, "I didn't factor in those cretins."

There was a banging from the bathroom and then Gus's voice saying, "Get me out of here!"

By the time I got him out, by the time I'd heard his story of how two men in balaclavas had bundled him in there, Zoe had somehow disappeared.

I ran up to the main gate.

"Did my friend leave?" I asked Samsoni.

"Ms. Huntington-Smyth?" he asked.

Despite everything, I couldn't help smiling.

"That's right."

Samsoni checked the book. "About five minutes ago, on foot."

I was about to go back home when something else occurred to me.

"Did a car leave not long before that?"

Again Samsoni checked the book.

"A white van, actually," he said.

"So you've got a license plate?"

"That's right," said Samsoni.

Reading from the book he said, "OMT437."

I guess I could've asked him to write it down for me, but that was looking too try-hard; he'd start thinking there was something going on.

And there was something going on, but I didn't want Samsoni to know that.

OMT437. OMT437, I said to myself, over and over again, trying to get it to lodge in my brain.

"Is everything okay? There was nothing stolen, was there?" said Samsoni.

"Everything's fine," I said, but as I walked back to Gus's house I soon realized how phony that statement was.

I guess I'd always believed Halcyon Grove when it claimed it was the safest place in the world. All that CCTV. Those high walls. Security guards like Samsoni.

But The Debt had just waltzed in and done what they liked.

No, it wasn't safe.

Nowhere was.

Not anymore.

IT'S A RAMBUTAN, YOU CRETIN

The next day, we had training after school, but my mind was elsewhere.

It was on a scooter flying through a KFC, a bemused Colonel looking on.

It was inside a bulldozer tooling down a half-finished road.

It was with men wearing balaclavas.

It must've showed, too, because Coach Sheeds took me aside and said, "Is there anything wrong, Dom?"

"No," I said. "Everything's fine."

"School's fine?" she said.

"Fine."

"Home's fine?" she said.

"Fine," I said.

Fine. Fine. Fine.

I don't think Coach Sheeds was totally convinced, though, because she said, "Maybe you're a bit stale. Why don't you take an early shower today?"

It felt strange having a shower by myself, with none of the usual stuff going on. No towel flicking. No your-momma jokes.

It felt so strange that I gave myself the tiniest of flicks with my own towel.

And I said, "Geez, Silvagni, your momma's so fat she got herself baptized at Sealands."

I caught the bus home. And as I walked past Imogen's house, my eyes, as always, were drawn towards her window.

The curtains were closed, but there was a light on. I thought of Imogen in there doing Imogen things and my heart did a cartwheel.

I took out my iPhone and composed a text: *im, i am thinking of you*.

My finger hovered over the send button.

"Do it!" I ordered, but my finger wasn't taking orders from anybody.

It moved down to the delete button and, letter by letter, obliterated the text.

I kept walking. When I saw Dad's Porsche 911 parked in our driveway I knew something was up. Because Dad, like most business-tycoon types, usually didn't get home until at least nine.

My immediate thought was that I'd been found out and the house was crawling with cops of all sizes, shapes and jurisdictions. Ready to accuse me of taking a bulldozer for a joyride. Of being in the plane with the Zolt. To match my DNA to that found in Mr. Jazy's Mercedes. To interrogate the truth out of my poor old granddad. To rip my alibi to shreds.

But as soon as I walked through the door I knew, thank goodness, that my pessimism was unfounded. Excited chatter, the chink of champagne glasses; there was an air of celebration. My parents, my grandfather, Gus, my big sister, Miranda and my little brother, Toby were gathered in the kitchen. There were other people, too. Fiona, Mom's PA, and the DeClerks from down the street.

"What's up?" I asked Mom.

"Oh, sweetheart, you haven't heard?" she said.

"No, I haven't," I replied, wondering what it could possibly be.

There was nothing Mom liked more than being the bearer of good news. Which is probably why she did the job she did, running the Angel Foundation, distributing some of the money Dad made to various charities.

"Toby's going to appear on *Junior Ready! Set! Cook!*" said Mom.

"Really?" I said.

"You know he's been going to the auditions?"

I did?

Yes, I probably did. It's just that my life had been a bit hectic lately. You know, trying to avoid having my leg forcibly amputated and that.

But I totally got why he'd been chosen. Toby was a pretty amazing cook. And obsessed with food. There was this thing on *Ready! Set! Cook!* where they had to identify all these weird ingredients and Toby knew them all, every time.

"It's a rambutan, you cretin," he'd scream, jumping up and down – well, his version of jumping up and down – in front of the plasma. "Why can't she see that it's a rambutan?"

And when the contestants were cooking he'd say stuff like, "Ohmigod, I don't believe it, she's put her pipe of tempered chocolate in the fridge!"

So he totally deserved to be selected for *Junior Ready! Set! Cook!* and have these people over to celebrate and have Dad come home early from work and have Mom all excited like she was, more excited than I'd seen her for ages.

And it wasn't as if Mom or Dad could brag about my achievements.

"You should see the lovely brand Dom has on his thigh!" That wasn't going to happen.

"If it wasn't for our boy Dom, Tristan wouldn't be in a coma." Neither was that.

"Dom's been taking driving lessons, you know. For a bulldozer." Ditto.

I found Toby and gave him a big-brother slap on the back.

"Way to go, Rambutan," I said.

He smiled at me, opened his mouth as if he was going to say something. But then he was engulfed by more admirers and whatever he was going to say remained unsaid.

When I walked through the sliding glass doors and outside, Gus followed.

"How'd training go?" he asked. "Hope that idiot isn't pushing you too hard before this race."

Having two coaches – one at school, the other at home – had always been tricky, and it seemed to be getting even trickier.

Yesterday, however, somebody had gotten into Halcyon Grove, broken into Gus's house and locked him in the bathroom, and here he was talking about training!

What in the blazes was wrong with Gus?

"Training was okay," I said, and as I did I realized that maybe Gus had it right, that in a world gone crazy it wasn't such a bad idea to do normal stuff.

We chatted a bit more about the race before Gus decided to go home.

I walked back into the living room.

"So I guess movie night's off, then?" I said to Mom, trying to keep the peeve out of my voice.

Friday night was always movie night and nothing was supposed to interfere with that, not even something as tremendously, incredibly amazing as *Junior Ready! Set! Cook!*

"Of course not, darling!" said Mom. "We're going to the later showing, that's all."

"That's good," I said.

In a world gone crazy it wasn't such a bad idea to do normal stuff.

THE JOHNNY DEPP MARKETING MACHINE

True to her word, Mom was able to get rid of all our guests and we were all set for movie night.

Just as we were about to get into the car Dad got this phone call.

Saying Dad got this phone call is a bit like saying Dad exhaled, or Dad inhaled, because Dad is always getting phone calls.

Getting phone calls is part of his autonomous nervous system.

I heard him say something about Coast Home Loans, and then he told us that he'd have to make some more calls and maybe he wouldn't make the movie, but he'd definitely see us afterwards.

I didn't really have a clue how my dad made a living except that he was some sort of business tycoon.

I did know that he was somehow involved in Coast Home Loans, because it had come up a few times in the conversations I'd overheard, or half overheard.

And I guess I pretty much took it for granted that he made a lot of money, that we lived in an amazing house, that I went to an expensive school.

And if this meant that he sometimes missed movie night, then we just had to live with it.

Tonight it was Miranda's turn to choose the movie.

And when she said *Alice in Wonderland* I sort of wished I could get a phone call about Coast Home Loans, too.

"*Alice in Wonderland*?" Toby and I replied in unison, because *Alice in Wonderland* had been out for a million years already.

Why go to the cinema and pay to watch a movie when you could download it for free?

"There's a Tim Burton retrospective on at the Palace," said Miranda.

What she was really saying was that there was a Johnny Depp perve-fest on at the Palace.

Like most sixteen-year-old girls, and all sixteen-year-old girl nerds, she'd been totally exploited by the Johnny Depp marketing machine. I don't even know why they bothered with movies – they could've just projected a photo of Johnny Depp for an hour and a half and all those swooning girls would've still paid to go. Then they'd Facebook each other, say what an extraordinary performance it was, what a great actor he is, how much they "luv hm."

So I wasn't keen to watch Johnny Depp Johnny-Depping all over the place yet again, but one of the rules of movie night was that you had to respect the choices of others, no matter how totally and absolutely crap they were.

But as soon as Alice disappeared down that rabbit hole, I was captivated. Even more captivated than I was during *Four Minute Mile* or *Born to Run: The Sebastian Coe Story* or even *Saïd Aouita: The Arabian Knight*. So captivated I didn't even notice Johnny Depp Johnny-Depping all over the place. So captivated I wasn't even irritated by the continual munching from the next seat as Toby worked his way through two buckets of popcorn.

Because *Alice in Wonderland* is basically about a kid who, through absolutely no fault of her own, is thrown into a topsy-turvy world where the normal rules do not apply anymore.

Sound familiar?

When it was finished we walked outside into the blaze of blinking, flashing neon, of people thronging the footpath, and I was still in a bit of a daze. But when I saw Dad standing there waiting for us, tall and handsome in his suit, Patek Philippe watch glinting on his wrist, I snapped out of it.

I had this rush of pride for my dad. Self-made man, business tycoon. Who still worked all those hours, went on all those overseas trips. I thought of Mom's charity foundation, all the people it helped, all the stuff it gave away. How it wouldn't exist without Dad. And I felt a bit guilty because I spent so much time with Gus now.

"Dad!" I said, running over to him.

I wanted to give him a hug, and I was going to give him a hug, but I didn't. Not there, on the footpath, under all those lights, with all those people. Instead, I shook his hand.

"How'd those calls go?" I said.

He smiled his dazzling smile.

"Life grants nothing to us mortals without hard work," he said, quoting some old Roman dude.

After he'd given Mom a kiss he said, "So, people, how do we rate the movie?"

"It was really great," I said.

"Somewhat disappointing second time around," said Miranda.

And Toby answered with a burp, the buttery smell of regurgitated popcorn filling the air.

"Where should we go for dinner?" said Dad.

Not Taverniti's, I thought. *Please not Taverniti's.*

"What about Taverniti's?" said Mom, utilizing her acting ability to suggest that this was a novel, possibly totally-out-there, idea.

"Taverniti's it is, then," said Dad.

We walked there, along the street, past theatres, restaurants, entertainment arcades. Past a gaggle of Japanese tourists taking photos of the famous Manny Hans neon sign. The sign itself wasn't anything spectacular, it was just an ad for a local firm of electricians, which said, in flashing blue and red, *Manny Hans Makes Lights Work*. But according to the *Guinness Book of Records* it was the oldest continually illuminated sign in the Southern Hemisphere. Nearby, a man in an Earth Hour T-shirt was handing out pamphlets.

"You guys didn't have much luck with this last year," said Dad, waving the pamphlet away, pointing to the sign.

Last Earth Hour some activists, armed with wire-cutters, had tried to sabotage the Manny Hans sign. They hadn't gotten very far, though. In fact, one of them had ended up in the hospital.

"Those idiots weren't associated with our organization," said the man.

"Didn't one end up with third-degree burns to the dreadlocks?" joked Dad.

All us kids laughed at our father's excellent joke, but the man didn't find it quite as amusing.

"Like I said, nothing to do with us."

As we kept walking Mom said, "We won't be here anyway."

"We won't?" said Dad.

"Bali, remember. The Plummers are getting married."

"Again?"

"It's a renewal ceremony."

"Another one?" said Dad, rolling his eyes.

"Then who's looking after us?" asked Miranda.

"Your grandfather," said Mom.

Almost immediately, Miranda had her phone out and was texting away. I knew exactly what she'd be saying, too. *bg prty my hse erth hr.*

As we approached Taverniti's a couple of disheveled-looking kids approached us, a boy and a girl.

There were always kids like this on the Coast. They were probably living rough, sleeping on the beach, cadging food.

It was only when they got closer that I realized that these were the kids I'd seen in the hospital yesterday when I was there with Zoe.

I averted my eyes, went into I-can't-see-you mode. So, I noticed, did Toby, Miranda, Dad, Mom.

When the girl said, "Can you spare some change for a bus fare?" none of us said anything.

But then the boy said, "Mrs. Silvagni?"

Mom quickened her pace.

"Mrs. Silvagni, it's me, Brandon? Remember?"

Dad threw Mom a look, and Mom stopped.

"Brandon?" she said. "Imagine seeing you back on the streets."

She switched into full-on professional mode and we had to wait while she called a few numbers, then put the kids into a taxi with instructions for the driver to take them to a nearby hostel.

"Happy now?" I thought I heard her mutter to Dad when she rejoined us.

But it was such a weird thing to say that I figured I must've misheard her.

There was nothing wrong with Taverniti's itself. It was a really nice restaurant with really nice food and really nice staff. And because they knew us, and knew that Dad was a generous tipper, we always got special personalized service.

"And will you be having three entrées again tonight, Toby?

"And are you excited by the new model iMac, Miranda?

"And how is your running career progressing, Dom?"

That sort of special personalized service. But whenever I was at Taverniti's I couldn't help thinking about Imogen's dad, about how he disappeared, dematerialized, vaporized from here on the day he was reelected to state parliament.

After we'd ordered from the waiter, Rocco Taverniti, the owner, came out to make sure everything was okay. Everybody on the Gold Coast knew Rocco Taverniti. Mostly it was because he owned the Gold Coast Tritons, our local soccer team. But he was also involved in lots of other stuff. He was about Dad's age, I guess. And he was handsome, too. Though in a more Italian way than Dad.

"*Buonanotte*," he said. "*Com'è la mia famiglia preferita?*"

"You know I don't speakka the lingo," said Dad, smiling, shaking Rocco's hand.

"You're a disgrace, you are!" said Rocco in a joking voice.

He talked soccer with Dad for a while, both of them agreeing that the Tritons needed a new striker for next season.

"There's a couple of Brazilians we're looking at," said Rocco.

Their conversation, as all conversations in the Gold Coast seemed to do, moved on to real estate.

"See Smithy paid seventeen mill for that place in Mermaid," said Rocco.

As they talked on I recalled what Mr. Jazy had said about what would happen when the housing bubble burst, how things would get "real ugly."

Then Rocco and Mom started talking about a new initiative of the Angel Foundation in which Taverniti's was going to offer apprenticeships to disadvantaged kids.

I tried to imagine Brandon in the kitchen wearing one of those chef's hats, but I just couldn't.

"If he's so rich," said Toby when he'd gone, "why does he still work in a restaurant?"

"Because he's a workaholic," said Mom, looking at Dad. "Just like your father."

A bottle of French champagne arrived at the table.

"Compliments of Rocco," said the waiter.

"Do you think Mr. Havilland is still alive?" I asked.

Mom gave me a don't-go-there look.

"Not this again," complained Toby.

Miranda rolled her eyes.

"As I've told you many times, I think it's possible," said Dad.

I imagined Mr. Havilland on a beach somewhere. But why would he leave Imogen like that? I re-imagined him on a beach somewhere, with total amnesia, so he didn't know he had a wife and a daughter, a daughter so beautiful that total strangers in linen suits armed with glossy business cards were desperate to make her the world's next supermodel.

"Tell us how you met again," Miranda said to Mom and Dad.

Mom squeezed Dad's hand. Dad squeezed Mom's hand. Mom made goo-goo eyes at Dad. Dad made goo-goo eyes at Mom. I could've killed Miranda.

Mom launched into the story.

"So as you know, I came out here to do a show in Sydney."

"*Les Mis?*" said Miranda.

"Yes, that's right – *Les Mis*. We were doing two shows a day, seven days a week, so when the run finished we decided that a vacation would be in order. In those days, of course, the Internet wasn't what it is today. So some of the other girls and I went into a travel agent's. And it was the first brochure I saw. Surfers Paradise. Beaches. Sand. Surf. Everything that a California gal like me needed."

"Come on, Mom," said Miranda. "Sing the song."

"Yeah, come on, Mom, sing the song," said Toby.

Please not the song, I thought.

Dad looked adoringly at Mom. *Sing the song.*

So Mom sang the song, in her big Hollywood voice, with her big Hollywood hair – well, the chorus anyway, all about California girls.

Everybody, of course, was now looking at us. A couple of people even clapped.

"Encore," yelled some moron.

"A week later I walked into this place," said Mom, indicating Taverniti's with a wave of her manicured hand. "Though it was only a small joint in those days, a hole-in-the-wall really. And there were these two good-looking men sitting at a table."

Now it was Mom's turn to look at Dad adoringly.

"They were a bit scruffy, perhaps, but still very good-looking."

This was the one part of the story I always had trouble with, because I couldn't, no matter how much I tried, imagine my dad as "scruffy."

"I need to go to the bathroom," I said.

Dad looked annoyed, like he thought I just didn't want to hear the rest of the story. And he was right, I didn't. Because the other good-looking but scruffy man sitting with Dad when Mom walked in that night had been the now-vaporized Mr. Havilland.

I ignored Dad and headed to the bathroom. Afterwards, instead of turning right to where my family was sitting, I turned left.

Don't ask me why, I just did. Or maybe I was thinking about Imogen's dad again, wondering how he could have just disappeared like that. I came to a door, so I pushed it and it opened into a narrow back alley.

"*Chi è?*" somebody said.

I closed the door behind me and now I could see that the voice belonged to an old man who was sitting on an upturned cooking-oil drum. At his feet were five or six tough-looking alley cats. He was feeding them cubes of salami, talking to them in Italian.

"Hello," I said.

He looked up at me. Now I recognized him: it was old Mr. Taverniti.

When I was a little kid he was the one who would greet you at the door, show you to your favorite table, tell you about the day's specials. I hadn't really noticed when he'd stopped doing this, when the next generation of Tavernitis had taken over, but they obviously had.

I remember thinking he'd been old back then. Now, I guess, he was ancient.

"*Issettiti*," he said to me.

"Sorry, I don't speak Italian," I said.

"Calabrian," he said, his voice creaky. "I am speaking the dialect from Calabria."

"Well, I definitely don't speak that," I said.

He patted the oil drum next to him and said,

"I asked you to sit down."

I did as he asked. He tossed the rest of the salami onto the ground and the cats squabbled over it.

After studying my face for a while he said, "And how is your grandfather?"

"My dad, you mean?" I thought that he couldn't be talking about Gus, because Gus didn't like eating out very much, especially not at Taverniti's; Gus hated Taverniti's.

"Giuseppe?" said old man Taverniti.

Okay, he had meant my grandfather, though Gus also hated being called Giuseppe. "That stupid peasant's name," he called it.

"So how do you know my granddad?" I said.

"He was a good runner."

"He was," I said, and then I added just about the only Italian I knew, "*Buon corridore.*"

"In Calabrian we say *fui bono,*" said the old man.

I gave that a go.

"Good," he said.

Suddenly the photo I'd seen that day in Gus's drawer flashed in my mind.

"So did you know my grandfather's brothers?" I asked. "The twins?"

"*Gemelli?*" he said. "The twins?"

"That's right," I said.

Old man Taverniti was looking right at me, with

63

eyes that seemed much younger than the ancient head they resided in.

He said something in Calabrian, softly.

"Pardon?" I said. "What did you say?"

I heard the door behind me creaking open.

"Dominic, there you are!"

I looked around to see Rocco.

"We've all been looking for you," he said. "Your entrée is on the table."

I'd rather have stayed here, found out what old man Taverniti had said, talked to him further, but Rocco just stood there, glaring at me, and I had no choice but to get up. As I walked back past the bathrooms I could hear old man Taverniti and his son talking in Calabrian. Of course I had no idea what they were saying, but it was the son who was doing most of the talking, and from the tone of his voice, he seemed to be telling his father off.

"Where were you?" said Dad when I got back to the table.

"Major dump," I said.

"Do you have to?" said Toby, his mouth full of bocconcini.

"This is a family dinner," said Dad, his voice tense. "And I think we'd all appreciate your company."

"Really?" said Toby.

Mom put a calming hand on Dad's hand. "It's

okay, dear. Dom's here now."

"Are you going to eat that, or what?" said Toby, his eyes on my calamari.

After dinner we walked back home, through streets that seemed brighter, more illuminated, more neon-infested than before.

SERIOUS GOOGLING

The next morning I did some serious googling.

First I typed in *Rocco Taverniti*.

As I'd expected, there was a lot of stuff about the Tritons. Article after article, photo after photo. A beaming Rocco Taverniti at the opening of the new Tritons stadium at Carrara. A beaming Rocco Taverniti with his arm around star Brazilian recruit Gonzaga. And a beaming Rocco Taverniti as part of the Australian bid to hold the 2022 FIFA World Cup. A couple of things soon became clear: Rocco Taverniti wasn't averse to publicity, and he really liked to beam.

But there was other stuff as well, because Rocco Taverniti seemed to be on every board of every organization in the Gold Coast. The Gold Coast Development Board, the Gold Coast Small Business

Association, the Gold Coast Italo–Australian Club. You name it, he was on it.

But what surprised me was that he also seemed to be involved in the Save Ibbotson Reserve campaign.

Could Rocco Taverniti possibly be a greenie?

It didn't take long for me to get sick of Rocco Taverniti and his beaming, so I typed *Graham Havilland*, Imogen's father's name, into Google.

Again, there were a lot of hits. I brought up the first website and began reading an old newspaper article. *Local politician and anti-drugs campaigner, Graham Havilland, disappeared from a Gold Coast restaurant in mysterious circumstances today…*

When I'd finished reading, I was just about to start on the next article when I had another idea.

I found Dad on the treadmill – he sure was putting is some serious kays lately.

"Can I ask you a question about Mr. Havilland?" I asked him after he'd finished, after the treadmill offered him its usual puerile encouragement: "Great workout! Champ! Hope to see you again soon!"

Immediately a concerned look appeared on his sweat-shiny face.

"Look, Dom, you might have to let go of the Graham thing," he said.

"Let go of it?" I replied. "I thought he was, like, your best friend."

Dad paused, as if he was getting his thoughts in order. Even then he made a couple of false starts, opening his mouth as if to say something, then closing it again.

Eventually, sick of impersonating a guppy, he said, "Graham made a lot of enemies in his time."

"Because he was against drugs?" I said.

Again it seemed to take Dad forever to answer.

"You have to remember that the Gold Coast has had, how should I put it, a colorful history. In fact, it used to be a bit of a Wild West sort of place," he said.

Dad had gathered himself some momentum now.

"Thankfully, that's all changed and I can pretty confidently say we've got the best lifestyle of anybody in this country, bar none."

"But what –" I started, before Dad cut me off, saying, "Let's not discuss this any further."

He went to put his arm around my shoulder, something he had done a million times before. But an image appeared in my head: Dad holding the branding iron, its tip glowing red. Then the pain. Then that smell, somehow, returned to my nostrils.

I couldn't help myself, I recoiled.

As I did, anger contorted my father's face, turning him into somebody no lifestyle program would ever want as its host.

But then it was gone, and he clamped his hand on my shoulder.

"You know I'm always here for you, Dom," he said, squeezing hard.

"I know," I said.

Now I wanted his hand to stay like this, but I knew it wouldn't because Dad was a very busy man, because Dad was always on the move.

Sure enough, with a glance at his Patek Philippe he said, "Better get a move on, got a conference call to the States happening," and he and his hand were gone.

"Great workout! Champ! Hope to see you again soon!" said the treadmill again.

"You're a moron," I told it.

Lights flashed.

"You wouldn't know what a great workout is," I told it.

More lights flashed.

Some of my fellow runners didn't mind running on a treadmill. Gabby, for one. And Bevan Milne could sit, turd-like, on a treadmill for hour after hour. I hated treadmills. Hated the fact that no matter how fast you ran, no matter how much effort you put in, you didn't go anywhere. Just stayed there looking at the TV, or some spot on the wall, or some meaningless figure on the console.

But when more lights flashed it seemed like some sort of challenge, so I stepped onto the treadmill and hit the start button.

"I'll show you a workout!" I said.

I pressed the pace button until it was at its maximum. Did the same with the incline button.

I started running. And I have to admit, I did have to put in some effort to keep up, to stop the machine spitting me out the back. But it wasn't long before I was bored. All that effort and where do you go? The same old place. I was just about to step off when the machine sped up.

How could that be? I looked at the figures on the console. I'd already bumped it up to its maximum.

Now it was quite a challenge and I had to really put in some effort to stay on.

"Great run!" said the treadmill. "But you haven't reached your second programmed goal! Champ!"

It was the same annoying California voice, but it seemed to me that there was a slight change in its tone, that somehow the treadmill was mocking me.

"You really are a moron," I said, between breaths.

The machine sped up even more.

Now I was pretty much sprinting. And freaking out: was the machine actually racing me?

It sped up even more.

Now I was running as fast as I could, maybe even faster than I could. And yes, I could've just jumped off, but that didn't really seem like an option.

But when it sped up even more, I thought enough was enough, and I hit the stop button.

It didn't stop.

I pulled out the emergency stop lever. It still didn't stop.

In fact, it sped up even more.

Time to get off, I thought.

But again, for some reason, I couldn't.

It was me who had challenged the machine.

So I kept pounding away, sheets of sweat dropping off me now, my heart thumping in my chest.

And then the machine stopped.

"Great workout! Champ!" it said.

And I couldn't help smiling at it. "Great workout!" I agreed.

But as I went to step off the machine it said something else, something that sounded like, "Turn off all the lights during Earth Hour!"

I told myself I was hearing things. Treadmills didn't say things like, "Turn off all the lights during Earth Hour." They said things like, "Well done!" or "Great workout!" or "Champ!"

But there again, this was no ordinary treadmill.

And when it said it again – "Turn off all the lights during Earth Hour!" – I knew that I really had heard correctly.

The Debt had spoken again. This was my next installment.

"But where?" I said to the treadmill.

"The Gold Coast," it replied. "For one hour only!"

"That's not possible!" I said, but that, apparently, was the end of our conversation.

Because despite asking it several more questions I received no answers.

I went back to my room, onto my balcony.

There were no clouds in the sky. The pool's surface was unbroken. I could just make out the remnants of our old fort, high in the fig tree. And the only sound, that of a distant lawnmower, ceased.

It was quiet, and it was still, and the anger was building inside me. Anger fueling anger.

The Zolt had escaped, hadn't he?

Gus had lost his leg to cancer.

ClamTop was a gimmick.

Like Alice I'd fallen into a topsy-turvy world where normal rules did not apply. A world that Dad and Gus, for some strange, perverse reason, had invented.

I picked at the edge of the scab on the inside of my thigh.

Don't! I told myself, but I kept picking until I'd raised the scab a bit and a smear of blood appeared.

Don't! I told myself again, but this time I listened to what I had to say and stopped picking.

"Hey you," I yelled at ClamTop. "You're not so talkative today, are you?"

Nothing happened.

"Are you?"

Moving back into the room, I brought my mouth so close it was almost touching the cool burnished metal.

"Are you?" I yelled.

There was no response. I took the ClamTop downstairs. I took it outside. And I put it in our trash can. Just to make sure, I piled some stuff on top of it so that it was buried deep.

PREACHER'S

The next day was unusually gloomy, the sky a patchwork of gray, a hint of rain in the air.

"Loose as a moose on the juice," said Seb by way of a greeting.

He was wearing a Bart Simpson T-shirt, and shorts that were even baggier than usual.

"What happened to the goose?" I said.

"Goose is on vacation," he said.

"Where do gooses, I mean geese, go on vacation?"

"Venice," replied Seb. "Gooses dig gondolas."

We both smiled at the silliness of it.

As we neared the bottom of the Gut Buster Seb's phone went off, playing a tune that sounded very heavy and very metal. I knew he always carried a mobile – I'd seen it jiggling around in his pocket – but this was the first time it'd rung while we were running and I was intrigued.

Maybe now I'd learn something about his family.

He answered in English, well, sort of English: "Yo, wassup!" but soon switched to another language. At first I thought it was Italian, but as his conversation progressed I changed my mind.

Calabrian? But it didn't sound like the language old man Taverniti and his son had been speaking.

Was it another dialect?

When Seb hung up, I asked him, "What language was that?"

"It's from the old country," he said.

"I realize that," I said. "But what language was it?"

By then we'd reached the Gut Buster and Seb said, "I'll tell you at the top."

He took off, and I mean really took off.

Let him go, one part of me said, *you're in a taper, you've got the state titles soon.*

But another part of me, a less obedient part, wasn't going to let that happen.

I took off after Seb.

Accelerating up a hill is one of the hardest things you can do in running, guaranteed to get your heart pumping, to get your heart thumping. And Seb was really putting in hard. It was only right at the end that I managed to catch him.

"Got ya!" I said.

As we cruised back down the hill, both of us sucking in the big ones, Seb said, "Hey, what say we mix it up today, have a run through Preacher's?"

Through Preacher's?

The Preacher himself is a pretty scary old dude. And then there are the bodies, the murdered, mutilated, moldering bodies they talk about at school. Supposedly, Preacher's Forest is littered with them. And the last time I'd been there it'd been in an airplane, with the Zolt. And that experience had made Preacher's even less attractive as a place to run, especially on a gloomy, golf-unfriendly day like this.

Seb must've seen the doubt on my face, because he said, "Come on, I'll show you a thing or two about cross-country running."

Show me a thing or two? I'd been on the cross-country team for two years before I'd switched to track running.

"If there's any showing to be done," I said, "I'll be the one doing it!"

Despite my boast, it was soon obvious that Seb knew Preacher's much better than I did. So I let him take the lead, following him as he made his way down one of the many narrow tracks that criss-crossed the scrubby bushland. I could smell the wood smoke well before we got there, before the track opened out and we were in a clearing, before we were at the Preacher's camp.

The Preacher, dressed in an overcoat, was hunkered over the fire. He looked up as we ran past, his eyes blazing from a face black with grime.

I'd never been this close to the Preacher before, never really seen his face before. And when I did I was surprised, because there was something about it that was familiar.

"The black riders of the Apocalypse are upon you!" he said, his strident voice shattering the morning stillness.

"Morning to you, too, sir!" Seb said to him, before looking at me, smiling.

I didn't find the Preacher as amusing as Seb did, however, and I was glad when we left him and his apocalyptic utterings behind.

We were now in a part of Preacher's that was wilder, more heavily wooded, where the track was rougher. As I ran, concentrating on the terrain, I started to wonder about the wisdom of what I was doing. Why was I risking spraining an ankle before such an important race?

"Bikes!" yelled Seb as he stepped off the track.

Preacher's Forest was very popular with mountain bikers. Invariably they thought they had the right of way. And us runners weren't going to

77

argue: they were bigger than us, more metallic than us. Three of them passed, on black bikes, in black leathers, with black full-face helmets.

"Wow!" said Seb. "Who were they?"

The Debt, I thought, remembering the motorbike riders who had picked the Zolt and me up after he'd landed the plane.

Seb increased the pace. I'd never run off-road with him before, but it soon became obvious that he was a natural. He literally never put a foot wrong, negotiating the rocky track as if it were a smooth hi-tech race surface. Despite my cross-country experience, I found it hard going, and a couple of times I stumbled before managing to regain my footing.

"Bikes," said Seb.

Again, he stepped off the track.

I did the same. This time there were no bikes, however.

"That's strange," said Seb. "I'm sure I saw one up ahead."

As he said this, there was the sound of a gun going off, and something – a dart? a bullet? – flew between Seb and me at about chest height. Another report, but Seb and I had both hit the ground and the projectile whizzed harmlessly over our heads. We got to our feet and took off, running back down the track, sprinting until we reached the Preacher's camp again. The Preacher was still there, still in his overcoat, still hunkered over the fire.

"Help!" I yelled. "You have to help us!"

The Preacher stood up, and now I could see that it wasn't the Preacher. Whoever it was, he was wearing black leathers. And there was a gun in his hands. He took aim, and shot. There was a needle-sharp pain in my thigh. A burning sensation that rapidly spread through my body. Before everything went black.

ESCAPE FROM WARD C

I snapped into consciousness and a woman I didn't know was leaning over me, smiling at me. Her blue uniform came into focus, the stethoscope dangling around her neck.

She must be a nurse. I must be in a hospital. And then another, more sinister, realization: it must have been The Debt who put me here!

"Why am I here?" I said, or attempted to say, because my mouth was dry, my tongue a caterpillar, thick and furry.

"Here, drink this," said the nurse, handing me a glass of water.

I took a sip but it had a strange metallic taste.

Suddenly I thought of Gus's story: how one minute he was swimming in the ocean, the next minute he was waking up in a hospital bed, with his right leg gone.

I wriggled my toes; they were there.

But I knew this meant nothing, because Gus could still wriggle the toes on his right leg, the toes that hadn't been there for more than fifty years.

My leg! Panic mounting, I tore back the sheet. "My leg!"

I was naked. But both my legs were there. The right one with the scab on the inside of the thigh.

"What's happening?" I said.

"You're going to have a little procedure," she said, putting the sheet back.

"A procedure?"

"An operation."

"What sort of operation?" I said.

I noticed now that the nurse had a syringe in her hand and I had a drip connected to my arm.

"The specialist will be able to explain all that to you," she said. "In the meantime, you need to get some rest."

When she started to press the plunger on the syringe I grabbed the drip and yanked hard – it came out.

"Now, young man," said the nurse.

But I was already out of my bed. The nurse hit the alarm button.

I grabbed a towel, wrapped it around my waist, pushed open the door and ran. Straight into the beefy arms of an enormous security guard. He squeezed me tight, but I managed to bring my knee up hard into his groin. He released his grasp a bit. I gave him the other knee in the same general area. He released his grasp a bit more, enough so that I could slip out of it and start running. Down one corridor, then another, then another. Not knowing where I was going. Not knowing if I was running from The Debt or into The Debt. I was just running.

Until I saw a green exit sign.

Until I was outside with only a thin hospital towel between me and a charge of gross public indecency.

A garbage truck rumbled past, trailing a thought-bubble of flies. I ran after it and stepped onto the bar at the back, hooking each arm around what looked like pistons.

The smell emanating from inside the truck was sickening. And the flies, obviously seeing me as some sort of competitor, were now dive-bombing me, trying to drive me away.

I could see more security guards hurrying out of the hospital doors, but the garbage truck turned around a corner and I was out of sight.

I'd thought – I'd hoped – that the garbage truck would continue to trundle around, picking up garbage, and I could've picked a convenient place to get off.

No such luck.

We were headed for the entry ramp onto the freeway. And we were going too fast for me to jump off.

The wind was now trying to rip off my towel. I unhooked one arm, holding the towel in place with that hand.

A car came up behind me, the driver an old lady with a halo of blue hair. I could see her eyes widen as she noticed me on the back of the garbage truck. I let go of the towel to give her a reassuring thumbs-up.

I'm okay, Granny.

But as I did the wind whipped the towel from around my waist.

I just managed to grab it before it flew away and ended up on the old lady's windshield. She gave me a smile and a thumbs-up of her own before she put on her indicator and shuffled over to the next lane.

Anzac Bridge, said the sign, and now I knew I was in Brisbane, that somehow The Debt had brought me here.

I knew why, too – they were flexing their muscles, punishing me for trashing ClamTop.

As we drove onto the bridge, the traffic slowed considerably.

And people started beeping their horns. Brisbane, and the Anzac Bridge in particular, is famous for its traffic snarls. But then I realized that some of them were beeping at me. And behind me, a man in a Lexus was on his mobile phone. A few minutes later there was the wail of a police siren. The traffic had slowed down to walking pace now and I knew it was time for me to lose my garbage truck.

"Bye, flies," I said. "It's been a buzz."

I stepped off the back, and, dodging cars, ran over to the side of the bridge. Unfortunately, I'd chosen the side that didn't have a footpath. Now, even more people were beeping their horns.

"Nice butt!" a woman yelled.

There were two police sirens wailing.

I looked over the railing, at the swirling waters of the Brisbane River below. It looked a long way down, but I didn't think it was that far, not jump-and-you're-dead far. The police sirens were getting closer, and somebody whose voice rang with authority yelled, "Hey, you!"

I climbed up onto the railing, the wind ripped the towel off, even more horns beeped, and I jumped.

It was further than I thought – I seemed to be in the air forever. And the water, when my feet hit it, felt like concrete, sending a judder through my whole body. My momentum kept taking me down, deeper and deeper, into water that was darker and darker. Eventually, my feet touched bottom. I kicked against it, but there wasn't much to kick against, just slimy mud. Eventually, when I was knee-deep in it, I stopped descending and slowly began to ascend.

I wasn't sure how long I'd been under, but now my lungs were burning. I looked up and could see the sun etched on the rippled surface of the water.

Not far now, I kept telling myself, kicking hard, grabbing rungs of water with both hands, pulling myself upwards, but my brain was complaining about the lack of oxygen and I was starting to feel light-headed.

Eventually, I broke the surface.

It was a state I was familiar with from running: the need to gulp in air, to replenish my lungs. When I'd finished I could see that I had another problem: the current was ripping along, and taking me with it, towards the open ocean.

I knew, having being caught in a few rips in the surf, that even if you're a good swimmer you don't try to swim against a strong current, you don't try to fight it. Because that was one fight that the current, undisputed world champion in all weight divisions, was always going to win. Even swimming across the current, making for either shore, wasn't advisable when it was ripping as ferociously as this. You'd soon tire, you'd soon drown.

Conserve your energy, settle back and enjoy the ride, Dom, I told myself.

Unfortunately, there wasn't a whole lot to enjoy. Yes, the water was warm but that was about it.

As I neared the open ocean, as the river widened, I thought the current would slacken off.

I was wrong. If anything, it became stronger. Relatively calm before, the water was roiling now.

I wasn't a competitive swimmer like Tristan, but I could swim a kilometer freestyle, no problem. And I could probably breaststroke all day if I needed to. So I was still confident that once the current released its hold on me I'd have the strength to make it back to shore.

That was until I saw the tanker. A great, giant brute of a thing, it appeared from behind some containers stacked on a distant wharf.

Keep going that way, I told it. *Don't come here.*

The bow heaved around, and the great, giant brute of thing was now headed directly for me. And what's more, I was headed directly for it. In fact, I was probably going faster than it was.

I knew that if I was anywhere near the tanker when it passed I would get sucked into its whirling vortex. Then there would be no escape – I would get carved up by its enormous propellers.

Why did I run away from the hospital?

Why did I get on that garbage truck?

Why did I jump off that bridge?

And then another question: why did I go to Preacher's in the first place?

But before I could answer that I saw it: about halfway to the left-hand shore was a navigation buoy.

A boo-ee, I thought, because for some weird reason I always saw buoys through Mom's American eyes.

The boo-ee was red, streaked with bird poo, with a shag sitting on top of it.

I knew that if I could somehow get to it, wrap my legs around its mooring chain, then I might have a chance against the tanker's fearsome suction.

So I started swimming.

Not towards the buoy, because then the current would take me beyond it, but towards a point on this side of it.

I put my head down and thrashed hard with my arms.

I was Tristan.

I was Ian Thorpe.

I was Michael Phelps.

And I missed the boo-ee by about a meter.

I watched it fly past, the shag throwing me a sympathetic look. I desperately tried to get back to it but it was no good. Not even Tristan, Ian Thorpe, or Michael Phelps could've made headway against that current. I looked up and the tanker was almost on me, the huge vee of its bow, its towering superstructure, the shuddering throb of its engines.

They say that just before you die, your whole life flashes before your eyes. They're wrong. Nothing flashed before my eyes. All I could think of was those dreadful propellers, slicing me up like the salami at Taverniti's.

And I thought of what Gus had said: "No creditor wants to destroy their debtors, because then there's no chance they can make their repayments."

Well, it looked like The Debt got this one wrong.

I didn't see the white unmarked Jet Ski until it was almost on top of me. The man driving was wearing a black wet suit, wraparound glasses and a cap.

He came alongside, leaned over, grabbed me by the wrist and yanked. He was immensely strong, and it felt as if my arm was going to pop out of its shoulder socket. It didn't, though, and I managed to scramble onto the back of the Jet Ski. There was a boom from the tanker's foghorn. The man twisted the throttle and the Jet Ski responded immediately, rearing up, then accelerating away. Another blast of the tanker's foghorn, but we were safe and I watched as the great steel wall, streaked with rust, passed us by.

"Oh my God, thanks so much!" I said, but my words were whipped away by the wind as the Jet Ski headed towards the shore.

When we were close, the man eased the throttle and we glided in towards a stretch of mucky sand.

"Thanks heaps," I said. "What are we going to do now?"

The man answered by twisting the throttle hard. The Jet Ski reared up, my legs flew into the air and I tumbled off the back.

I sat on the muddy bottom, oily water lapping my waist, and watched as the Jet Ski, gathering momentum, headed back upriver. Even when it had disappeared from view I didn't move. I moved my focus to the tanker, watching until it too had disappeared. It was only when a dead fish, its silvery belly distended, floated past that my brain seemed to start working again.

Did all that really happen? Had I really almost been killed?

It seemed that after such a momentous experience I should be having feelings, emotions, that were equally momentous. But I wasn't. Sitting there, water washing around me, dead fish floating past, I felt extraordinarily calm, more calm than I could ever remember feeling before. And I probably would've stayed there, except that I suddenly realized crabs were nipping at my extremities, fingers, toes, all of them.

I got up and waded to shore, thinking about what to do next. I was buck naked and a long way from home. It seemed to me that I should do something about the former before I tackled the latter. The beach – if you could call it that – was littered with debris, layers and layers of it; it looked almost post-apocalyptic, the earth choking on all this crap.

Surely, I thought, among all this stuff, there had to be some clothes here, something I could wear.

I was right. Sort of. There was clothe. Singular. A skirt. Pleated. Tartan. Filthy. But I put it on, using a piece of frayed yellow nylon rope as a belt, and set off.

Behind the beach there were mangroves. I stood at the edge, looking at the mud, smelling the mud.

Beyond it, I could hear the faint rumble of traffic.

I thought of that rhyme my kindergarten teacher used to sing to us when I was a kid, the one about going on a bear hunt.

Oh no! Thick yucky mud.

Can't go over it. Can't go under it. Got to go through it.

Squish. Squish.

Squish. Squish.

At least there were no crocodiles, I assured myself. Not this far south.

So I started squish-squishing through the thick yucky mud towards the sound of the traffic.

As I walked, more pungent smells seemed to erupt out of the mud. Mosquitoes attacked me, penetrating my skin, my blood their Frappuccino.

Can't go over it. Can't go under it. Got to go through it.

Up ahead I could see an embankment, on top of it a road.

Almost there, I told myself, just as I saw the crocodile.

Well, that's what I thought it was, but of course there weren't any crocodiles this far south.

It was actually a tractor tire, half buried in the mud, which had managed, somehow, to make itself look like a croc.

Still, I ran – stumble trip stumble trip – all the way to the embankment, scrambling up its rocky side until I was on the road.

As traffic whizzed past, I thought about sticking out my thumb. I quickly decided against it, however – there would be too much to explain. *Right, so you thought they'd chopped off your leg?*

So you hopped onto the back of a garbage truck? And then you jumped off the Anzac Bridge? And a tanker almost ran you over?

Forget it.

But then a taxi pulled up in front of me and the driver leaned out of the window.

"You look like you might need a ride," he said with an accent.

"Luiz Antonio," I said, remembering the name I'd read a few weeks ago on the license.

He smiled and said, "Hop in."

So I did.

I was so grateful that he'd picked me up that I didn't want to think too much about what a coincidence this was: what, he just happened to be driving along this road?

"Can you take me to the Gold Coast? Halcyon Grove?" I said. "I don't have any money on me, but I can get somebody to pay you when we get there."

"Sure," he said. "Not easy to carry a wallet when you're wearing something like that."

Okay, I suppose it was pretty funny, but I wasn't exactly in a laughing mood.

"No, it's not," I said, smoothing my skirt over my thighs.

We took off, and he switched the car stereo from radio to CD mode.

The music that started playing was very rhythmic, heavily percussive.

"You like samba?" he asked.

"I don't know much about it."

"It's from Brazil," he said.

I remembered that last time he'd picked me up he'd said that he was from Rio.

He sang along to the CD.

"What does it mean?" I asked.

"Basically, if you don't like samba, you've got a bad head and sick feet."

I laughed at that, glad for anything that took my mind off what I'd just experienced.

"I suppose I like samba then," I said. "So you're from Rio, right?"

"Cidade marvilhosa!" he said.

As Luiz Antonio drove he told me about Rio de Janeiro, about the beaches, the football, the carnival.

I'm not sure when I fell asleep, or how I could fall asleep with samba playing, with him talking, with all those itchy mosquito bites, but I did, and when I woke up we were at the Halcyon Grove gates and Samsoni was peering in through the window.

"Everything okay, Mr. Silvagni?" he was saying.

"Sure, fine," I said.

Apart from the fact that if I didn't get ClamTop back from the trash The Debt would probably cut off my leg.

Samsoni didn't look convinced and I couldn't blame him.

"Some mates pranked me pretty good," I said.

Samsoni smiled at that.

"Do you mind fixing up the driver? I'll pay you back later," I said. "I really need to get home."

"Of course not," said Samsoni, taking out his wallet and extracting a twenty-dollar bill.

"It's actually two hundred and seventy-three dollars," I said, reading the meter.

Samsoni gave a low whistle, put the money back into his wallet and went to hand the driver his credit card, but Luiz Antonio waved it away.

"I was coming down here anyway," he said.

I tried to argue with him but it was no good; he didn't want my – well, Samsoni's – money.

"Do you have a card?" I said, figuring that if I had his details I could work out a way to get his money to him.

"Sure," he said, taking a card from his top pocket and handing it to me.

"My house is that way," I said, pointing to the right.

As Luiz gently eased his foot off the clutch and

we chugged off, I couldn't help myself. "Can you please step on it, driver?"

"You're the boss," said Luiz Antonio.

He stepped on it and the taxi responded by backfiring twice and then slowly gathering momentum.

By the time my house came into view I already had my hand on the handle.

"Thanks," I said as I got out, the car still rolling.

"No problem," he said.

Readjusting my skirt, I ran straight for the trash can. I threw open the lid. It was empty!

Immediately I imagined the worst: ClamTop in a vast landfill. ClamTop compacted. Me in a vast landfill. Me compacted.

"Master Silvagni," came a voice from behind me.

I turned around.

It was Roberto, the head gardener, the one who didn't actually do any gardening. In his hand was a bag, one of those green environmentally friendly shopping bags.

"Yes," I said, trying to inject some authority into my voice, not easy when you're wearing a filthy, pleated tartan skirt kept up by a piece of frayed yellow nylon rope.

"I'm pretty sure this is yours," he said, holding out the bag.

I peered inside. It was ClamTop.

Immense relief, but then several questions occurred to me. Where did he get it? How did he happen to be there exactly when I got home? And the big one: did Roberto, our head gardener, have something to do with The Debt?

"Where did you get this?" I said.

"Take it," he said, and there was this tone in his voice, as if he was somebody who was used to telling other people what to do, and I don't just mean telling the junior gardener to mow the front lawn.

When Dad talked to the staff he sounded almost apologetic, as if he wished he didn't have to ask them to do things. Mom, however, never said "please" or "thank you"; she just gave unambiguous orders in her big American voice.

"But I asked you where you got this," I said, adopting some of Mom's born-to-order tone.

Roberto didn't answer and there was this sort of Mexican standoff, the two of us standing there, eyeballing each other, the ClamTop inside the shopping bag between us.

Eventually Roberto broke eye contact and said, "I found it, Master Silvagni. And Hue Lin said it was yours."

Hue Lin was the cleaner; she was often in my room, so it made sense that she knew ClamTop was mine.

So maybe he was telling the truth, maybe he did find it, maybe he didn't have anything to do with The Debt after all.

I took the bag.

Was about to say "Thank you" but decided not to.

"By the way, Roberto?" I said instead.

"Yes, Master Silvagni?"

"I reckon the grass around the pool needs edging," I said.

"I'll see to it myself, Master Silvagni," said Roberto, before he turned around and sauntered off.

I hurried inside and upstairs to my room. I realized that there was less than a week until Earth Hour!

What an idiot I'd been. Only a few days for me to work out how to do the impossible, how to turn off all the lights on the Gold Coast.

I had a shower and got changed into clean clothes.

Then, with a spiraling sense of urgency, I powered up my desktop, got online and started googling.

Lights. Electricity. Power. I googled everything and anything that came into my mind.

I knew it wasn't the way to tackle a problem like this. I knew I should be approaching it slowly and methodically. But I couldn't help myself. With the terrifying sound of those throbbing engines still in my ears, I kept frantically googling, website spawning website, breeding exponentially like bacteria.

Then my phone went off.

Charles calling … So I answered it.

"Hey, where are you?" he said.

Though Charles Bonthron was on my running team, I wouldn't exactly call him a friend. However, the familiarity of his voice served as a sort of circuit breaker.

I looked at my computer screen: there were websites swarming all over it, literally hundreds of them.

"I'm home," I said, slumping in my seat.

"Doing what?"

"Nothing," I said, which couldn't be closer to the truth. I was doing nothing except wasting what little time I had left.

"We were supposed to work on our civics project, remember?"

"Civics?"

"Yes, civics. 'The History of Sewerage in the Gold Coast,' that sort of thing."

"I've got an idea," I said.

"You have?" said Charles.

"What about –" I started, before I was interrupted by a *rat-a-tat-tat* on my door.

"Hey, can you just hang on a sec?" I asked Charles.

"Sure," he said.

"Who is it?" I said, my hand over the phone's mouthpiece.

"Toby's on television in fifteen minutes," came Miranda's voice from the other side of the door. "It's probably a good idea if you were there to watch it."

"Okay, thanks," I said, and returned to my conversation with Charles. "Like I said, I've got this idea …"

GREEN TEA AND LYCHEE

When the first judge from *Junior Ready! Set! Cook!* took a spoonful of Toby's green tea and lychee ice cream, a look of absolute pleasure appeared on his large round face.

He opened his mouth and said one word, drawing out all the syllables, as if they too were to be savored slowly.

"Ex-tra-ord-i-nary."

"Toby, my darling!" Mom yelled at the screen.

And later when the three judges gave my little brother three perfect scores of ten, our living room, packed with various friends of my parents, erupted into applause.

My hands were working as hard as anybody else's – clap, clap, clap. Actually my hands were probably working harder than anybody else's – CLAP,

CLAP, CLAP – compensating for the fact that inside I actually wasn't feeling so happy-clappy.

I was genuinely pleased for Toby. How could I not be? Three perfect scores – that was totally kicking culinary butt! But wasn't I in a sort of contest, too? One in which the stakes were a fair bit higher? But nobody was allowed to clap for me.

When the clapping receded, and I felt as if I could safely let my arms drop to my sides, Miranda took one of my hands and squeezed.

She knows, I thought. *She's an amazing sister*.

"We are so lucky to have such a talented brother," she said.

Right then, I missed Imogen.

Missed her so much it ached.

I couldn't tell her about The Debt, about all my accomplishments, but what I could say was something throwaway like, "Geez, Toby and his rambutans," and she'd say something like, "Yeah, I know exactly what you mean," and that would be enough: I'd feel better.

When they announced that Toby had made the next heat there was even more applause.

My phone rang.

It wasn't a number I knew.

I answered it anyway. "Hello."

"Hello, Dom," came a fractured voice over the phone.

"Yes, who is it?"

"It's me, Mr. Jazy."

Immediately the world simultaneously expanded and contracted. All the people talking about Toby, what a culinary genius he was, what a future he had, were now miles away. But the voice emanating from the phone seemed incredibly close.

"I'm calling from the hospital," said Mr. Jazy.

I could hear my own voice say, "Is Tristan okay? Is he okay?"

There was nothing from the other end but crying, but sobbing.

"No!" I yelled, and everybody's eyes were on me.

The sobbing at the other end stopped and Mr. Jazy said, "He woke up, Dom. My son woke up!"

First Mom was going to drive me straight to the hospital, but then she decided that she had to see her guests off first. And then Dad was going to do it, but he decided he'd better help Mom. In the end Gus said he'd drive me. And Miranda, for some reason, decided that she'd come along too.

I'm sure there are slower drivers than Gus in the world. The recently deceased, for example. Or the legally blind. And yes, I know the old chap only has one leg, so I shouldn't be so mean. But as soon as Mr. Jazy said those words, "My son woke up," I wanted to be there, wanted to see Tristan awake.

His exterior, not just his interior, alive.

I almost wished it was Hound de Villiers who was behind the wheel, spurring Gus's old truck through the traffic. Besides driving at an excruciatingly slow pace, Gust also insisted on talking about the upcoming race. Apparently he'd been on the phone – or "the blower" as he insisted on calling it – talking to some old running contacts of his.

"These Kenyans," said Gus. "They're running sub-fours."

My brain, my mind, whatever it is that deals with this stuff, registered the fact that these Kenyans were running sub-fours, which was at least a second faster than my PB.

I wanted to react, say something to Gus like, "Wow, that's going to make it tough."

But my brain, my mind, whatever it is that deals with this stuff, had moved on and was now screening a short film titled *Tristan and Dominic: The Highlights*.

There was Tristan moving in next door to Imogen, strutting around like some kind of rock god. There was Imogen and me coming up with our saying: Rap is crap, sharks are cool, under no circumstances should dads ever be allowed to wear Speedos and Tristan Jazy is so not okay. The pile-driver punch in the guts. Me sucking up to Tristan, getting him to invite me to Reverie Island. Finding the Zolt's lair. Getting shot at. Tristan dropping me overboard. And then, finally, the crash. Fade to black.

"I hope it's not temporary," I said. "I hope he doesn't lapse back into a coma."

Gus gave up after that and the only sound in the truck as we crawled along the road was Miranda tapping away on her iPhone. When we got to the hospital Gus refused to pay the exorbitant rates in the parking lot, so we ended up driving around and around the block looking for a spot. And when we eventually did find one, it took Gus ages to reverse the truck back into it. By the time we walked into the hospital I was sure that Tristan had lapsed back into his coma. Or had succumbed to old age. But as we exited the elevator on Tristan's floor, I knew I was wrong. There were people everywhere. And they were smiling, chatting away.

They must be relatives, friends of the Jazys, I thought.

Somebody said the word "miracle." Not once but twice.

And I knew then that he was still awake. But now I felt reluctant to go any further, to intrude.

Siobhan, the Irish nurse, saw me through the crowd and beckoned me over.

"Tristan has been asking for you," she said.

Asking for me?

Mr. Jazy appeared.

"Dom," he said as he enveloped me in a bear hug, except Mr. Jazy wasn't the bearlike being he used to be and his ribs were like little elbows.

Leaving Gus and Miranda in the waiting room, I followed Mr. Jazy into Tristan's room.

It was crowded inside. Mrs. Jazy was there, of course. And Tristan's sister, Briony. And some older people I assumed must be his grandparents.

And there, sitting on one side of Tristan's bed, was Imogen.

Imogen!

I smiled at her. Tristan was awake now, surely she couldn't keep blaming me for whatever it was she was blaming me for?

And in return I got … well, I wouldn't call it a smile; it was more like the seed from which a smile grows. But it was something, and if I'd been feeling good before, I was feeling gooder than good now.

As I moved closer to the bed I could see that Tristan's face was still pale, but it was no longer so pale it was lost in the white pillows that propped him up. And all the machines seemed quieter now; there was less blipping and beeping.

"Tristan, Dom's come to say hello," said Mr. Jazy.

Tristan turned his head until he could see me,

and he had this look on his face, like he was trying to work out who I was. If humans had hard drives, then his would have been whirring like crazy. But then there was a smile, which surprised me, because I'd always thought Tristan was only capable of smirking.

"Hey, come here," he said, patting the bed.

The other people in the room moved aside, creating a passage for me.

I perched on the edge of the bed, right next to where Imogen was.

Tristan grabbed me by the hand, squeezed it quite hard, as if to make sure I was real. I wanted to pull my hand away, but when I looked up at all the faces smiling at me, I knew I couldn't.

I wasn't sure who had cast me in this role, but I sure hadn't ever auditioned for it, and now that I was in it, I wasn't sure of my lines.

"It's really excellent that you woke up," I said. "I'm pretty sure you won't have to catch up on all the homework you missed."

This got a couple of laughs from the audience. Not from Tristan, however. Again I could hear that hard drive whirring.

Finally, in a half whisper, he said, "Those jerks really did shoot at us, didn't they?"

Immediately my eyes traveled around the room.

Nothing was registering on anybody else's face except Imogen's – she was the only other one who had heard Tristan's words.

"What jerks?" I said, keeping my voice low.

"Those rednecks on Reverie that day," said Tristan.

I knew that if I said no, that if I told Tristan that he'd imagined it, then Imogen would probably believe me. Tristan would probably believe me as well. He'd been in a coma for twenty days; who knew what crazy weird stuff had been going on in his subconscious.

But who was I to deny him the truth? Actually, who was I to deny myself the truth?

"They sure did," I said.

Tristan smiled at me.

Smiled, not smirked.

"Jerks," he said.

And when I looked up, Imogen's face was like stone.

No smile.

No seed.

Just the stoniest of stone.

My hand in my pocket, I surreptitiously took out my iPhone. Unlocked it. Tapped on the Fake-A-Call app. A second later my iPhone rang. I answered it, pretended to listen for a while.

"Yes, Mom," I said, injecting a note of urgency into my voice. "I'll be home straightaway."

"Great to see you, Tristan!" I said. "But I have to go."

I removed my hand from his and walked quickly out of the room.

THE EXCURSION THING

Mr. Ryan, our civics teacher, liked to do the high-five thing. Liked to tell you about the gigs he'd been to on the weekend. Liked to look you bang in the eye and talk to you as if you were his equal.

Mr. Ryan was also a runner. The 8-kilometer cross-country record he set when he was fifteen, and a student at this school, is still standing.

You'd probably think that cross-country running and track running would stick together, make a united front against cricket, football, swimming, those glamour sports that demanded all the funds.

Wrong.

Basically we hated each other. They called us the Track Rats, because we ran around and around in a circle, like rats on a treadmill. Supposedly. We called them the Mud Skippers, the Muddies for short, because they liked to run through filthy, leech-infested creeks.

And they were always trying to poach our runners.

I knocked on the door to his office.

"Come in," he said.

He was sitting at his desk, plugged into his iPod, a pile of papers in front of him.

"Hi, Mr. Ryan," I said, making sure I didn't get close enough for him to do the high-five thing.

"Dom," he said, removing the iPod buds from his ears. "You heard the new Dire Straits album?"

"I thought they were dead," I said.

"Ah, so you're more of a Guns N' Roses man, are you?"

"I thought they were dead, too," I said, though this wasn't strictly true because I'd seen Slash, or Slush, or whatever he called himself, on television the other night, plugging hair product.

"So tell me, what's boppin' ya pod these days?"

"Can we talk about the civics project?" I said. "Charles and I have decided what we want to do."

"You have?" he said, not even bothering to disguise the surprise in his voice.

"We have," I said, doing a bit of the look-you-bang-in-the-eye thing myself.

"So which one?" he said as he consulted a piece of paper that listed all the topics.

"Actually, I've come up with my own. I'd like to do the production and distribution of electricity."

"Electricity?"

I wasn't surprised that he was surprised: I wasn't exactly famous for the originality of my civics project topics. Usually I'd leave it to the last minute, until the only thing remaining was "The History of the Roundabout in the Gold Coast Municipality," or something equally scintillating.

"Did you know that all electrical generators work the same way?" I said. "Basically it's just a piece of metal moving between magnetic poles."

"Yes, of course," said Mr. Ryan.

"Did you know that the Diablo Bay Nuclear Power Station generates all the electricity for the Gold Coast?" I said.

"I'm well aware of that," he said.

My intuition told me that here was the time to stop. That no teacher wanted a student telling him stuff, especially a dud student like me. And, more importantly, no Mud Skipper wanted a Track Rat telling him stuff. But I couldn't help myself: I was seriously excited by electricity, charged by electricity.

"But do you know how it works?"

"Of course I do – there's a nuclear fission reaction that produces electricity."

"Sort of," I said. "The nuclear power is actually used to heat water which produces steam that turns the turbine that drives the generator that makes the electricity."

Mr. Ryan glared at me, a teacher–student glare, a Muddie–Rat glare, and waved the piece of paper in front of my face.

"Unfortunately, these are the topics that are stipulated by the curriculum," he said. "And there's not much I can do about that."

It was the old my-hands-are-tied, I'd-love-to-help-you-but-I-can't, and once a teacher goes into that mode, there's usually no shifting them.

Except for one thing: Seb.

I'd been thinking about my running partner quite a lot since Sunday, and every time I had I'd arrived at the same unsavory conclusion: Seb had set me up, he'd lured me to Preacher's.

Right now, though, I needed him.

"Seb looked pretty amazing in that trial," I said, remembering how Seb had told me that Mr. Ryan had approached him after and told him he'd have more chance of a scholarship with the cross country team.

At the mention of Seb's name, Mr. Ryan's nostrils twitched. A predator with the sniff of prey.

"So you and Seb spend some time together?" he said.

"I run with him every morning," I said, which was pretty much the truth.

"We've become very good friends," I said, which was sort of the truth.

"For some reason, he always listens to what I have to say," I said, which wasn't the truth at all, but it worked.

"Electricity," said Mr. Ryan, putting the piece of paper away. "It really is a fascinating topic, isn't it?"

"It sure is," I said. "Especially with an excursion tomorrow."

"Excursion?" said Mr. Ryan, alarm in his voice.

All teachers hate excursions. Hate having to get the permission notes, collect the money. And then the excursion itself. The endless head counts. All the things that can go wrong.

"It's okay, my dad is going to send a bus with a driver. So you don't need to collect any money."

"I don't?" said Mr. Ryan.

"And I've already got the permissions," I said, taking out a sheath of notes from my pocket and putting them on his desk. "These are the kids in civics who'd like to go."

"They are?" he said.

"And I've already spoken to Mrs. Curie, the PR person at Diablo Bay. All she needs is an official request from the school for a tour of the facility.

Here's her email address." I handed Mr. Ryan a piece of paper.

"She does?" said Mr. Ryan, looking at the piece of paper.

I could see that he still wasn't convinced, however.

"And Seb is coming along," I said.

"But he doesn't go to our school," said Mr. Ryan.

"I know, but I talked to Mr. Cranbrook. He thought it was good idea to give a potential scholarship kid a taste of what we have to offer at Grammar."

"Dom," said Mr. Ryan. "You really have covered all bases, haven't you?"

He held up his hand, and – why not? – we did the high-five thing.

ZE
TRANSFORMER

I was pretty sure the eight students who were waiting with me and Charles and Mr. Ryan for the bus to arrive weren't as interested in electricity, or nuclear power plants, as I was.

They just liked buses (Brent Fowler) or excursions (Chris Montgomery) or hated schoolwork so much they would take any opportunity to get out of class (the other six).

When the bus arrived, Marcus, Dad's Jamaican driver, behind the wheel, Brent Fowler got very excited.

"Wow, a Vantare Platinum Plus!" he said.

A man, immaculate in black pants and white shirt, greeted us as we boarded.

"Hello, my name is Leonardo and I'll be looking after your beverage requirements this morning," he said. "As you can see, we have an espresso machine so I'd be happy to take your order now."

The Vantare Platinum Plus was catered!

At first, I felt a bit embarrassed – Dad, it's a school excursion, not a transatlantic flight – but that didn't last long. Not with everybody saying how cool it was, not with everybody ordering coffees. Even Mr. Ryan was impressed.

"Do you do a decaf soy latte?" he asked Leonardo as he sat down next to me.

"Yes, of course," said Leonardo. "And we do have a choice of soy milk today: either the Organic Bonsoy or the Rainforest Alliance."

I directed Marcus to pull up outside Big Pete's, but there was nobody there.

Mr. Ryan looked at me – *where is he?*

"We're early," I said, looking at my watch, and we were early, by about three seconds.

Yesterday when I'd called Seb, when I'd explained to him that I'd fail this subject unless he showed, he'd said, "Daddy Bear, I'll be there."

"School's not a problem?" I'd said.

"School's never a problem," he'd replied.

Daddy Bear had believed him, too. But now I was asking myself why. He'd set me up, hadn't he?

I'd been almost turned into hamburger because of him.

Suddenly he was standing there, as though he'd materialized out of thin air. He was dressed very conservatively – for him, anyway – in jeans and a T-shirt, his hair tied back.

"I told you he'd show," I said to Mr. Ryan.

As Seb boarded the bus and sat down in the seat in front of us, Mr. Ryan's smile got bigger and brighter.

"Seb, can I get you a coffee?" Mr. Ryan asked him.

By the time we turned off the highway, following a sign that said *Diablo Bay Power Station 12km – Authorized Entry Only*, everybody had drunk at least two coffees each. And they were talking quite a lot.

"Has anybody ever had three triple shots in a row?" Kenny McCann asked Leonardo.

We'd left the last gated community behind and were now passing a cemetery, the Gold Coast Necropolis. There were the usual jokes.

"Dead center of town."

"People are dying to get in."

But I didn't find them funny. I hated any cemetery, even if it was called a necropolis. I hated cemeteries so much that last year, after I'd totally freaked out at some great-uncle's funeral, Mom had taken me to see a psychiatrist.

His name was Dr. Juratowitch and he smelled like mints.

"Your son is suffering from what we call 'coimetrophobia,'" he said, writing the word out in cursive with a fountain pen on a piece of paper, and handing it to me. "A morbid fear of cemeteries. Probably because they remind Dom of the finite nature of human existence."

"Is there anything we can do?" Mom asked.

"About the finite nature of human existence?" said Dr. Juratowitch.

I could tell that he was joking, but not Mom.

She wasn't really into jokes, or joking. Though she did laugh a lot during *Australia's Funniest Home Videos*. Especially when some kid on seesaw copped it in the knurries. Or a bride in a meringue dress capsized during the bridal waltz.

"No, about Dom's phobia," she said.

Dr. Juratowitch considered Mom's question for what seemed like ages, before he said, "No, not really."

I'd kept the piece of paper, though, and occasionally I'd take it out from my desk. Look at the word. Mouth the word.

It was a relief when the Gold Coast Necropolis – and my coimetrophobia – passed, replaced by green rolling hills.

Suddenly the bus stopped.

"Moo," said somebody near the front.

"Hello, girls," said somebody else.

I stood up to get a better look. There was a line of cows, the type with big swinging udders, crossing the road, moving between two gates, one on either side of the road.

Two women in overalls and gum boots were giving them directions, politely suggesting that they might like to get a move on. The cows, however, seemed in no hurry. And it was ten minutes before we could get going again.

Almost as soon as we did, though, we had to stop again. All the coffee that had been imbibed was now being unimbibed and the bus's toilet – or restroom as Leonardo liked to call it – wasn't coping with the demand, so we pulled into a rest area.

After we'd gotten moving again we turned onto another narrower road and the landscape changed. The hills flattened out – they were neither green nor rolling – and there were no more animals, none of the slow-moving udder-swinging domestic variety anyway.

All this time Mr. Ryan hadn't stopped extolling the extraordinary benefits of cross-country running to Seb.

We turned a corner, passed an abandoned roadside stall that had once sold *Fresh Tomatoes* and there they were, stalking the plain like huge steel orcs, their shoulders hunched, their knuckled hands clutching wires.

I couldn't help myself. "Look, transmission towers!"

Despite their caffeine intake, nobody was as excited as I was. Not even when the road passed right next to one.

Each of those wires carried 500kV of electricity, I wanted to tell them. Five hundred kilovolts!

"Imagine if that tower fell down," said Seb.

What was he, some sort of mind reader, or something? Because that's exactly what I was imagining. The tower toppling over, the wires touching, twisting, a flurry of sparks, of smoke, and the mother of all short circuits.

"Sorry?" I said, wondering if I'd heard him correctly.

"If that tower fell down," said Seb, "it would probably black out the whole of the Gold Coast."

Probably? It *would* black out the whole of the Gold Coast because, as I'd learned from my research, those four five-hundred-kilovolt lines were the grid's main power source.

But for how long? And that was my problem. Taking down the grid would be difficult enough. But taking it down for exactly an hour? That seemed almost the definition of impossible.

"Actually," Seb said, "the tower wouldn't even need to fall down. These kids I know made this miniature hot air balloon, right? Because they wanted to see how high their cat could go. They made it with, you know, wire in it. And it got caught in the power lines and, zappity-doo-dah, it blacked out the whole city."

I didn't want this conversation to go any further – it was way too spooky – but I couldn't help myself.

"Was the cat okay?" I said.

Seb shook his head. "They buried it in a matchbox."

I looked out of the window, towards the horizon, where four plumes of smoke billowed upwards, like gigantic white champignons.

Ω Ω Ω

"So as you can see, Seb," said Mr. Ryan, "the cross-country thing is a great option for you, especially if, as you said, you'd like to pursue your academic ambitions at our school. Of course, as you probably know, our facilities are second to none."

"Any last coffee orders?" asked Leonardo.

We pulled up at a checkpoint; a high fence topped with razor wire stretched away on either side.

"Hey, dude, has anybody ever done four triple shots?" asked Kenny, his voice skittering like a top across a table.

"I think you've had quite enough coffee, Kenny McCann," said Mr. Ryan, back into full-on teacher mode.

A square-jawed security guard boarded the bus and walked down the aisle, regarding us with a high degree of suspicion, as if each of us wore a turban and a beard and bore an uncanny resemblance to the late Osama bin Laden.

"To infinity and beyond," whispered Kenny McCann, and I couldn't help laughing because he was spot on: this security guard looked just like Buzz Lightyear.

"What's so funny?" said the security guard, glaring at me.

Now I noticed the holstered gun on his hip.

"Surprise can come from any direction!" whispered Kenny.

Again, I couldn't help laughing.

The security guard's hand was now on his gun.

"Do you consider national security to be a laughing matter?" he said.

"No, sir, I certainly don't," I said, glaring in Kenny's direction.

The security guard didn't move, however. Now I wished he was Buzz Lightyear, because Woody's best friend would never do that, scare the crap out of a fifteen-year-old kid with his shiny black gun.

"I have all the paperwork here," said Mr. Ryan, waving some papers at the security guard.

The security guard's hand moved off his gun and into his pocket. It came out with a camera, which he pointed at me.

Click!

"You're now in our database, punk," said the security guard before he snatched the papers from Mr. Ryan.

In their database – that was the last thing I needed. I could've killed Kenny McCann. I mean, really killed him.

We were allowed to pass through the checkpoint, and after ten more minutes of driving, high fences on either side, we came to the power station itself.

Mrs. Curie was waiting for us outside.

"Ze nuclear power plant is ze prime terrorist target," she said, in an accent so French I thought for a while that she was putting it on. "So we must all pass through ze scanner."

We did as she asked, passing through ze scanner, but when it was my turn, it buzzed.

"Belt? Watch? Rings?" asked the female security guard.

"No, none of that," I said.

"Pacemaker? Surgical pins?"

"No!" I said.

"Step over here, please," said the grim-faced guard.

I did as she asked, and she scanned my body with a hand scanner. This time there was no buzz.

"It happens," she says, waving me on my way.

"It is such a pleasure to 'ave you children 'ere today," said Mrs. Curie as she swiped her access card to let us through a secure door.

I could see that despite the caffeine-induced hyperactivity of some of my classmates, she really meant it.

And that's why it was a bit embarrassing when Chris Montgomery said, "Doesn't this facility produce large amounts of radioactive waste, some of which remains dangerous for hundreds of thousands of years?"

But Mrs. Curie had an answer all ready and raring to go.

"In zis age of global warming ze nuclear energy is ze cleanest energy available."

Okay, it was a politician's answer, one that didn't really answer the question. But still, she seemed very nice.

"And aren't there a lot of people who would like to see this facility shut down?" said Chris Montgomery. "Especially the diving community, who would like the marine area opened up again."

"In a democracy like zis, zat is zeir right," said Mrs. Curie.

Again, a politician's answer.

And fortunately Chris Montgomery didn't pursue the matter.

We were not allowed to get very close to the nuclear power station itself, but that was okay with me. It wasn't as if I was going to target it, to be responsible for my own private Chernobyl.

But when Mrs. Curie said, "I don't suppose you children would like to see ze transformer?" my ears pricked up.

"Probably not," said Mr. Ryan, who had already had a few terse words with Kenny McCann and was probably keen to get him and his excessive caffeine intake back on the bus.

"Actually, I'd quite like to see ze transformer," I said, unintentionally mimicking Mrs. Curie's accent.

Mr. Ryan gave me a look, and who could blame him? I'd never been the most enthusiastic student, but here I was, enthusing all over the place.

"I could meet you all back on the bus in half an hour," I said. "I'm sure Leonardo will have lunch ready."

"No problem," said Mrs. Curie. "I will bring 'im back."

Mr. Ryan agreed to this – it was, another opportunity for him to ear-bash Seb.

So I followed Mrs. Curie down more polished corridors, through more secure doors, CCTV cameras recording our every step.

Who was I kidding?

A crack terrorist unit with a mandate from their god would have difficulty breaking into here, let alone a fifteen-year-old kid. Eventually we came to ze transformer. Again, there wasn't that much to look at. Another room, full of computers. Two more operators – one male, one female – sitting in front of consoles. Reading from screens, tapping at keyboards.

"So you want to know what's happening here?" asked the male operator, who Mrs. Curie introduced as Gabriel.

"Sure," I said. "What's happening here?"

Gabriel pointed to a window, through which ze transformer itself, a large black box with a spaghetti of wires coming in and out, was visible.

"What that bad boy does," he said, "is knock down the juice from the reactor to something a bit more manageable."

"To five hundred kilovolts," I said.

"Top of your class, kid," said Gabriel. "But what we also do here is monitor demand from the grid. You see, the thing with juice is that it's not easy to store. So when the grid wants more juice, we give it more juice. You just don't mess with the grid."

Like The Debt, I thought. Because you don't mess with them, either.

"So, it's all just run by computers," I said.

Gabriel, I could see, wasn't pleased with this.

"Well, it isn't actually, mate. There's an operator override on everything. Computers are all well and good, but a computer doesn't know, like I do, that tomorrow night the Mariners are playing the mighty Tritons, and half the city will be tuned into the game. Do you know how much juice it takes to run a plasma?"

Guiltily, I thought of all the plasmas in our house.

"A lot?" I said.

"A heck of a lot. So before kickoff, we'll give the reactor a tickle, get it to squeeze out some more juice. Then we'll have no problems, no brownouts."

"How do you do that?" I said, and as soon as I did, I wished I hadn't.

The question sounded too bald, too pointed. Gabriel had no problem with it, however.

"It's all numbers, son," he said. "I input them here and they get shunted up to the plant."

As he said this I noticed the wireless router sitting beside his console.

"So if you wanted to, you could turn the power off for the whole of the Gold Coast?" I said, and again I couldn't believe how stupid I was, asking such a question.

Gabriel smiled at me, shrugged his shoulders, said nothing. But it was the smile and the shrug of a man with the power to turn off the power for the whole of the Gold Coast.

We stood there for a while longer, admiring ze transformer.

"You order pizza?" I heard Gabriel ask the other operator.

"It's Wednesday, isn't it?" she replied.

"Well, I think our time is up," said Mrs. Curie, checking her watch.

After thanking Mrs. Curie profusely, I moved off to join the others in the bus.

As I boarded the bus, Leonardo handed me a meal tray, like you have on airplanes. Unlike airplane food, this food was actually delicious. I'm sure even Toby would've approved.

On the way home Marcus put some reggae on the bus sound system.

And because Leonardo wasn't just a bus waiter but an actor and a musician and a multimedia installation artist, he organized a sing-along. Everybody was into it, especially Kenny McCann.

As we stopped to turn onto the highway, a scooter turned off the highway and headed towards Diablo Bay Nuclear Power Station, the rider wearing the distinctive blue-and-yellow uniform of Big Pete's Pizzas.

"No woman, no cry," sang Kenny McCann, his enormous, completely out-of-tune voice filling the bus.

TAI CHI, TO FU AND WI-FI

As I dived into the pool, I thought of my recent dip in the somewhat less sparkling waters of the Brisbane River.

It didn't seem possible that all that stuff really had happened to me. It had, though, and somehow a clean, but tattered, tartan skirt had turned up in one of my drawers just to remind me.

I intended to swim the whole twenty-five meters underwater, a feat I'd achieved countless times before. But when I got about halfway something strange happened – my throat constricted? my lungs deflated? – and I had this feeling that right there, right then, I was going to drown. In my own pool, in a meter of water, and there was absolutely nothing I could do about it. I would open my mouth and the water would pour into my body and I'd drown.

Of course, drowning was a bad thing. But it was also a good thing, because if I drowned I wouldn't have to deal with The Debt.

I opened my mouth and water did pour in, but I immediately closed it again and forced myself, spluttering, to the surface.

I hoisted myself onto the side of the pool and lay there on the warm deck, eyes closed, trying to understand what had just happened.

"I can't believe they would cook prawns for over an hour," came Toby's booming voice.

I opened my eyes.

Miranda, dressed like a ninja warrior, was doing her tai chi exercises. While Toby, not dressed like a ninja warrior, was stretched out on a lounge chair, a cookbook balanced on his belly.

"There should so be some sort of law against that!" said Toby.

Yes, there should be, Toby. But there isn't. So there's no use whining about it.

I got to my feet, walked closer to Miranda.

"Hey, is it easy to hack into a Wi-Fi network?" I asked her as she went into the Swooping Goose move.

I was no expert on tai chi, but this looked like an excellent Swooping Goose.

"I mean, they'd be just mush," said Toby.

"Easy-peasy," said Miranda, knees bent, arms outstretched.

Easy-peasy for her because she was a computer genius, but what about mere techno-mortals like me?

"Really?" I said

"Even half an hour would be stupid," said Toby.

"I could write you a sniffer program in ten minutes flat," said Miranda, moving out of the Swooping Goose and into the Squatting Panda.

Problem was, I couldn't get her to write a sniffer program in ten minutes flat, even if I wanted to. The Debt, and its rules: no help allowed.

"Maybe they expect you to keep the shells on," said Toby. "But then they should say that – prawns with shells on!"

"For Pete's sake, Toby, can you stop talking about prawns for five seconds?" I said.

"Look who's talking," said Toby. "The cross-dresser."

"Sorry?" I said.

"Mom said I could borrow some of your socks, and I found your little number hidden away in your bottom drawer."

"My socks are in the top drawer!"

I looked over at Miranda; did she have any idea what he was talking about? No, she was too busy concentrating on the tricky opening to the Irate Macaque.

"Whatever!" I said to Toby.

"Whatever!" repeated my little brother, and I have to admit he could out-whatever me any day he liked.

He closed the book, got up clumsily from the lounge chair.

"Oh yeah, big brother. With your coloring, I'd steer well clear of tartan," he said, before he waddled off.

"Whose network do you want to break into, anyway?" said Miranda.

"Nobody's; it was just a, you know, theoretical question," I said.

Miranda smiled a knowing smile. "Well, theoretically, there's a heap of stuff on the net," she said, giving me the name of a website.

As I walked back across the lawn, I asked myself if I'd already told Miranda too much. I even took a quick look around, made sure there was no punishment on its way. Then I realized how crazy that was, how I was becoming as paranoid as Gus and Dad. As silly as Gus and Dad. How would they, The Debt, know what I said to Miranda? They weren't godlike, they weren't omniscient, able to see everything, hear everything.

"You good?" came a voice from behind me.

I spun around. It was Roberto, the non-gardening gardener. It was the first time I'd seen him, up close anyway, since he'd returned the ClamTop.

Unusually he was holding a tool, a pitchfork, its surprisingly sharp prongs glinting in the sun. I stood there, transfixed by them, imagining what damage they could do. To muscle. To tendon. To cartilage. To sinew. To me.

I forced my eyes away and said, "I'm good, Roberto," before I hurried inside.

Back in my room, I powered up my iMac and went straight to the website that Miranda mentioned. She was right about there being a heap of stuff available. It was like the outraged hackers of the world had risen up and united against the common scourge of the secure Wi-Fi network. I downloaded a PDF entitled "The Secrets of Wi-Fi Hacking" and began reading.

It started off with a quote: "Every matter requires prior knowledge," attributed to To Fu, a fourteenth-century Chinese warrior king.

Yeah, right on, To Fu!

The opening chapter was all about WLAN and WPAN and WWAN networks, 802.11 and 802.15 protocols, and it didn't make a whole lot of sense to me. I persevered, though – just as I'm sure To Fu would've perservered seven hundred years ago in his quest for prior knowledge – rereading the chapter several times until I thought I knew what it was about.

As soon as I read – or tried to read – the first sentence of the second chapter I knew I was in trouble.

Now you have discovered the closed ESSID, bypassed MAC address filtering, cracked WEP, perhaps circumvented higher-layer defenses such as the deployed VPN …

Trouble that even a fourteenth-century Chinese warrior king couldn't get me out of. I kept reading, though. Kept trying to understand. But the words were no longer making sense, the letters that comprised them squirming like worms. The more I looked, the more I tried to concentrate, the more vigorously they squirmed. Until the whole screen was just compost, a mass of squirming worms.

Who was I kidding?

Me, a hacker? Yeah, sure.

"Stuff you, To Fu!" I yelled, and other less polite things.

I slammed the iMac shut. As I did, ClamTop cracked open. The screen flickered into life and the words *LOCAL WI-FI NETWORKS* appeared at the top of it.

Below it was a list of names, network names.

Some of these I recognized because they were the same local networks that came up on my computer. There were more of them, however, indicating that the ClamTop had a much greater range than it did.

But when I had a closer look at them, it seemed that all the networks belonged to people in Halcyon Grove, so my guess was the range was about two kilometers.

The top one, SILVAGNINET, was our network at home. I could log into that one, because I knew the password, but most of the other networks were locked.

Still, using the tip of my finger I scrolled down the list, highlighting each network in turn, until I came to HAVILLAND, the network in Imogen's house. There was a little padlock symbol next to it, which meant it was secure. So even if I wanted to join HAVILLAND, I couldn't, because I didn't know the password.

"You're not so smart after all, are you?" I told ClamTop.

Immediately, a red cartoon devil appeared in the middle of the screen, clutching a trident. Below it flashed the words *cracking password* ... The devil began dancing, hopping from one cloven foot to the other, thrusting its trident into the air. After about twenty seconds *cracking password* ... became *password cracked* and the devil had a devilish smile on its devilish face.

Now I could see that there were two computers connected to the HAVILLAND network: MOTHERSHIP and SYLVIA. I knew SYLVIA was Imogen's laptop because SYLVIA was what she called all her computers. I tapped SYLVIA with my finger. It highlighted. I tapped it again. The screen went black before suddenly coming to life again.

It took me a while to understand what I was looking at. And when I did, I almost had to look away. Because it was a clone of Imogen's computer, of her desktop!

Photoshop was open, in it a photo taken at what looked like some sort of political rally. People with arms linked, people holding placards. About half of them, starting from the left-hand side of the photo, had colored faces. I watched as the cursor hovered over another person's face, watched as this face suddenly turned light blue.

Now I got it: it was the same thing Imogen did with the photos in the newspaper; she was looking for her dad. I continued watching, mesmerized, as the cursor moved on. When she'd finished, when all the faces were different colors, I could feel the tears swimming in my eyes. The photo was so sad, all these people who weren't her dad, who would never be her dad, no matter how long and how hard she looked, but it was also beautiful, in a weird sort of way.

Imogen closed Photoshop and brought up Windows Mail. Again, I looked away. *You have no right to be here,* I told myself. *You're a dirty hacker. You're a perve.* But my eyes were drawn back to the screen.

Imogen started typing a new message.

Ruby, I have decided that this email petition I've attached is the best way to get them to turn off the lights in Halcyon Grove for Earth Hour, she wrote.

I picked up my phone, scrolled through "Contacts" until I came to Imogen's number.

My thumb hovered over the dial button.

Should I?

Shouldn't I?

Should I?

Shouldn't I?

There was no way I could make a decision, not for something as important as this, so I decided to let somebody else make it for me.

In this case, the fly that was perched on the window ledge.

If that fly moves within the next ten seconds, I'm going to call her.

Ten. Nine. Eight. Seven. Six. The fly lifted its wings.

And flew off, making several buzzing loops before it disappeared outside.

The fly had spoken.

I hit dial.

I imagined Imogen's phone, on Imogen's desk, playing Imogen's favorite ringtone.

And playing.

And playing.

And playing.

The fly had spoken, but the fly was a moron – this was humiliating.

Because I couldn't say, well, she's not answering because she's having a shower, or because she's having a swim. I knew she was there, checking her emails. No, she wasn't answering because it was me calling.

The kid who had put Tristan in a coma.

Who hadn't told her that we'd been shot at.

And then she answered.

"Hi," she said.

Okay, it may not have not been the most enthusiastic "Hi" in the history of "Hi," but it was a "Hi" nonetheless.

139

And it was an Imogen "Hi," the first one I'd heard in weeks.

"Hi," I said, trying to inject a bit more pep into my "Hi," but that wasn't easy – it's always the first "Hi" that sets the tone. "It's great about Tristan, isn't it?"

"Of course it's great," she said.

And then there was silence, so I said, "I'm thinking of getting a petition up this year about Earth Hour. It was disgraceful what happened in Halcyon Grove last year."

More silence at the other end, and I wondered if I'd gone in too hard.

But eventually Imogen said, "Dom, that is totally freaky! That's exactly what I was just doing."

"No way."

"Way," she said, and now she sounded like the old Imogen.

"In that case, can you send the email to me?" I said. "I'm sure it's better than mine."

"Of course."

When she hung up, I turned my attention back to the screen, to Imogen's cloned desktop.

The "Forward" button lit up.

I turned to my iMac. Opened Thunderbird, my email client.

Downloading 1 message of 1, it said.

Imogen's message appeared in the in-box.

I leaned back in my seat, arms crossed across my chest. It was starting to dawn on me exactly what I had here, how powerful it was. It was like a Dummy's Guide to Hacking, except it went out and actually did it for you.

But is that all it can do? Is that all I can do?

I went back to ClamTop, to Imogen's desktop. She'd minimized Windows Mail and was now starting on another photo in Photoshop.

Using my finger, I double-tapped the Windows Mail icon. It worked, Windows Mail opened! I maximized it so that it took up the whole desktop. I picked up my phone, called Imogen again.

She answered with, "You again."

"Is your computer okay?" I said.

"Sure, it's fine."

"And you're looking at it now?"

"Dom, I'm looking right at it and it's totally fine."

I double-tapped on "Compose New Message."

A virtual keypad popped up on the screen.

"So it's not doing weird stuff?" I said as I tapped my address into the recipient field.

"The only one doing weird stuff is you," said Imogen.

For the message itself, I just tapped in some random stuff.

"You're sure?" I said.

"Are you okay?" said Imogen. "Has some alien life form taken over your brain or something?"

"I'm fine," I said, as I tapped send. "Hey, your email petition looks pretty cool."

I turned my attention to my iMac. Clicked on the "Get Mail." The message from Imogen appeared in my in-box, the random stuff I'd written. It said, *Dom I love you.*

I felt sort of intoxicated, giddy with the power I knew I now had.

"So can you sign the petition tonight?" said Imogen. "And then forward it to everybody you know?"

"I wouldn't worry about it," I said.

"Why not?" said Imogen, sounding annoyed. "I thought you were going to help me with this."

"The lights will go off," I said.

"You should hear yourself, you sound like somebody from a Harry Potter movie."

"Trust me, Imogen. They're going to go off."

"Not unless we do something about it, they won't, Lord Voldemort. And do you know what's even weirder? You're the second person today who's told me not to worry about it, that the lights are going to go off anyway."

"Really?" I said "Who was the first?"

"A man from Fiends of the Earth."

"Who are they?"

"They're this greenie organization. I guess you could say they're pretty radical. They're the ones that liberated twenty thousand battery hens last year. I called them because I thought they'd have experience with setting up email petitions. Anyway, the person on the phone told me not to worry because the lights were going to go out anyway."

Just then, Imogen's desktop played a tune. She had mail.

Again, I couldn't help looking.

I sort of wished I hadn't.

guns&sixpack@hotmail.com had to be Tristan.

"So has Tristan signed your petition?" I said.

"Who?"

"Tristan?"

"What made you say that?"

"Well, he lives in Halcyon Grove, doesn't he? I was just wondering if he'd already signed your petition."

There was silence at the other end, a lot of silence, until Imogen said, "Tristan's just woken up from a coma."

I looked at the screen, at Windows Mail, at Tristan's unopened message.

Don't do it, I told myself.

You'll regret it, I told myself.

I did it, and I immediately regretted it.

cant stp thnking of u, said the message.

"Hey, I've got to go," I said to Imogen.

I hung up. I threw my phone on my bed. Then I threw myself on my bed. And I started crying.

Which seemed pretty ridiculous to me. A tanker had almost turned me into sashimi and I hadn't even come close to losing a tear.

Yet here I was, a human sprinkler.

There was a knock on my door, but before I could say anything like, "Go away!" or "Rack off!" Miranda entered.

"How'd you do with that Wi-Fi thing?" she said, but as she came closer, she must've seen my tear-irrigated face, because she said, "Dom, what's wrong?"

I couldn't talk to her about The Debt, but this wasn't The Debt, so it was almost a relief to be able to say, "It's Imogen. Her and Tristan are going out together."

"How do you know that?" she said, kneeling by the side of my bed, putting her hand on my shoulder. "Did she tell you?"

"Not exactly, but I know, okay."

"Hmmm," said Miranda, and she was quiet.

The slight pressure of her hand felt good, it felt

reassuring, and my sprinkler stopped sprinkling.

Eventually Miranda said, "I guess the problem with you guys is that you've been friends for such a long time and that's how you think of each other: as friends, not boyfriend and girlfriend."

"Then why was I crying?" I said.

"Because what you think and what you feel aren't always the same thing," said Miranda.

"Wow!" I said. "How do you know about this stuff?"

"Hey, I'm a girl," said Miranda. "Plus I watch a lot of movies."

"So what should I do?"

Again Miranda seemed to take ages to answer. "It's a tough one. Tristan's a bit of a tool, but Imogen's got the right to hang with him if she likes. And she probably feels sorry for him, after what he went through."

You traitor, I thought. This was not what I wanted to hear.

Miranda continued. "As far as you and Imogen go, maybe you'll have to stop being her friend before you can become her boyfriend."

Again I couldn't help saying, "Wow!"

"Girl, remember," said Miranda. "Plus movies."

BREAKTHROUGH PIZZA

"Dom!" yelled Coach Sheeds through the bullhorn. "What the blazes are you doing out there?"

Thinking, that's what I was doing. ClamTop, for all its extraordinary power, had one major limitation: range.

I'd worked out that the furthest away it could pick up a network was about two kilometers. However, the security fence around the Diablo Bay Power Station was at least five kilometers from the transformer itself. I had to get inside that fence. But how in the blazes – thanks, Coach – was I going to do this? Tunnel under the fence? Parachute over the fence?

"Dom, pick up the pace!" shouted Coach Sheeds. "You're on sixty-fives!"

We were doing what Coach called "anaerobic training."

Four hundred meters at sixty-five seconds, then two hundred meters of jogging, then four hundred meters at sixty-five seconds again, and so on.

Unfortunately, if you're training anaerobically, your brain isn't getting its fair share of oxygen, and you can't think properly.

So I was taking it easy, running aerobically, diverting oxygen from oxygen-hungry muscles to oxygen-hungry brain.

And Coach Sheeds wasn't happy.

"Dom, I said pick it up!"

I did as she asked, I picked it up, lengthening my stride.

Which meant no more thinking.

As I passed Rashid on the bend he said, "Pizza!"

And Rashid said "Pizza" in the same way that I imagine a vampire would say "Blood."

"Pizza!" I replied, trying to emulate Rashid's passion, but it was no good. I liked pizza, but I didn't love pizza, and it showed, because my "Pizza" was nowhere as vampiric as Rashid's.

We showered and got changed and moved up to the Doug Bonthron Room, named after Charles's great-uncle, the one who'd won bronze in the mile at the Auckland Commonwealth Games. The walls were covered in honor boards; there were cabinets full of trophies. Again, the Bonthron name dominated. I wondered if Charles ever felt this pressure, the need to make sure the engraver never forgot how to spell "Bonthron."

Mr. Cranbrook, the principal, was already there. Shiny suit. Shiny face. He gave an over-enunciated speech in which he talked about the great tradition of distance running at our school. He talked about our achievements. The achievements we were yet to achieve.

When he told us that the state titles were a great opportunity to, and I quote, "enhance the school's brand," Charles caught my eye and we exchanged smiles. After the principal had finished it was Coach Sheeds's turn to talk.

There was no Hakuna Matata. No "pain is inevitable, suffering is optional."

She seemed uncharacteristically nervous. Maybe the locker room gossip was true: if she didn't get results this season, Coach Sheeds was going to get the old heave-ho.

After she'd finished, there was a knock on the door.

"Pizza!" said Rashid.

"Blood!" said Dracula.

He was right, the door opened and three pizza delivery guys entered, wearing the distinctive blue-and-yellow uniform of Big Pete's Pizzas, carrying the distinctive blue-and-yellow boxes of Big Pete's Pizzas.

The cheesy, yeasty smell of pizza took over the room.

"Come on," said Rashid, fangs bared.

But I didn't move.

Because I realized I knew how to do it, how in the blazes I was going to get on the other side of that security fence.

FIENDS OF THE EARTH

The Fiends of the Earth worried me.

I'd done some research and found out that Imogen was right, they'd claimed responsibility for the "liberation" of twenty thousand battery hens from a farm near Ballina.

LET CHICKENS RUN FREE, they'd spray-painted on the side of the shed in red letters two meters high.

That most of the liberated chickens had subsequently been eaten by wild cats, or had drowned in creeks, or had been flattened by cars, didn't seem to have worried the Fiends of the Earth. Chickens had run free. For a while anyway.

Although they hadn't claimed responsibility, they were also suspected of being involved in several other acts of ecoterrorism. There was the firebombing of the offices of a live-sheep exporting business. There was the sinking of a Japanese longline boat while it was berthed in Cairns Harbour. And finally there was the sabotage of logging machinery in Far North Queensland, in which a logger, asleep in the back of a grader that was blown up, suffered severe injuries.

We had this reggae band at school. They were a crap band – I reckon people should need a license to play reggae and that license should be a) very expensive and b) very hard to get – but they had a great name: The Reckless Zealots.

Well, that's exactly what Fiends of the Earth seemed to me: reckless zealots. And they worried me. Because if they did intend to bring the grid down, then I was pretty sure they weren't going to be very subtle about it. Not given their chicken-liberating, logger-maiming track record.

I found their number on the net and called.

"Good afternoon," answered a woman with an English accent. "Fiends of the Earth."

"I was calling about the upcoming Earth Hour," I said.

"Well, that's not our initiative," she said. "Though we support it, of course."

I changed the subject to battery hens, and it soon became obvious that this was something the woman was very passionate about.

"So where is your office exactly, if I wanted to come and get some material?" I eventually managed to ask.

"Most of it is available online," she said.

"I sort of prefer hard copy," I said. "All my friends think I'm really old-fashioned like that."

"We're in Nimbin. The same little mall as the Hemp Embassy."

"Nice," I said and hung up.

She'd sounded so calm, so reasonable, neither reckless nor a zealot, that I told myself I was worrying about nothing.

But then I remembered what Imogen had said and a scene played out in my head: a transmission tower toppling in a flurry of sparks, the grid down for days on end.

I called the number again, hoping that the man Imogen had talked to would answer this time.

But it was the woman with the English accent again.

"Hi, it's me again," I said, before I proceeded to regurgitate most of what she'd already told me about the immorality of keeping hens in cages.

Eventually she interrupted, still in that same calm, reasonable voice, "Look, you're not a cop or anything, are you?"

"No, definitely not a cop," I said, but it did occur

to me that maybe I should be behaving like one.

On TV, when cops question a suspect, they'll sometimes come straight out and ask them if they're the murderer, or the rapist, or whatever.

"Would you like a cup of tea?" Immediately followed by, "Did you kill Daphne McFadden?"

So I thought I'd try that tactic.

"Actually, I wanted to know if your organization intended to bring down the grid during the upcoming Earth Hour," I said.

A pause, and then the woman said, "Like I've already told you, though we support the initiative, it has nothing to do with us."

It was the same calm, reasonable voice but there was something different about it and immediately I knew she was lying. Don't ask me how, but I did.

I had no choice – the next day, I had to get myself to that same little mall as the Hemp Embassy in Nimbin.

TO DITCH THE UNDITCHABLE SCHOOL

The next day, when Mom dropped Toby and me off at school, I gave her a peck on the cheek and joined the throng of students heading for the entrance with its high tensile steel gates and cluster of CCTV cameras.

Once through those gates, once inside those lofty stone walls, there was no easy way back out. Not unless you were on some type of excursion, or the final bell had sounded at three-twenty. Coast Boys Grammar had always prided itself on its security, for being unditchable, for being The School That Can't Be Ditched.

And since Jason Walker had gone and gotten himself kidnapped, the security had been beefed up even more.

There were now six security guards or, as the

school preferred to call them, SPOs (Student Protection Officers), on duty: two at the entrance, two at the drop-off zone and another two who floated between these areas.

Dawdling, I waited until Mom had driven off. I even let Toby shuffle past me.

Now I could put my plan into action. Frantically patting my pockets, I exclaimed, "Oh no, I left my iPhone behind."

I was pretty sure this little performance wasn't going to win me the lead in the school play – thank God – but it gave me the excuse I needed to turn around and head back towards the drop-off zone, to where a gray Mercedes had just pulled up.

The door opened and Charles got out. Our eyes met, and he was about to say something but I held my finger to my lips. *Shhh!* He understood, and said nothing as he grabbed his bag from the backseat and started walking to the gate.

I ducked behind the car, pretty sure that the SPOs hadn't seen me. Now was the tricky part: I had to get across the Gold Coast Highway, across four lanes of traffic. And I had to do it without causing any beeping of horns, any screeching of brakes, any sickening thud as metal collided with flesh, anything to get the attention of the SPOs or necessitate the calling of an ambulance.

Because it was peak hour the traffic was moving quickly and continuously; if I waited for a break I would be standing here for the next hour.

On your mark! I told myself, imaginary starter gun in my hand.

Get ready!

Go!

As a middle distance runner, I probably didn't have the most explosive of starts, but I was across the first lane easily. The second lane was a bit more difficult, as there was an oncoming bus and I had to make a split-second decision as to whether I ran in front of it or waited for it to pass. I opted for the former and, fortunately for me, there was no irate beep of a horn. Now the traffic was coming from the other direction. I had to stop, as the third lane was almost bumper-to-bumper.

Stay here and eventually I was going to get cleaned up.

I had to go for it.

Suddenly, between a huge 4WD and a concrete mixer truck, there was a gap.

It's mine, I thought.

I raced into it, and through it, my momentum taking me into the fourth and last lane. Where a motorbike, the rider's helmet yellow with red flames, was bearing down on me, was almost on me.

Stay still, I ordered myself. *Let him evade you.*

I stopped, closed my eyes and made myself as small, as unhittable, as possible.

Whoosh!

The motorbike brushed past.

Opening my eyes, I sprinted to the footpath, down a side street and into a park. Kids were getting pushed on swings, kids were sliding down slides, while their mums – and a few dads – drank coffees.

The first glitch in my plan: the public bathroom where I was going to get changed, the one I'd so cleverly located on Google Earth, was locked. I couldn't very well get changed in the open, not with all those little kids around. I could imagine the chorus of disapproval. "Stranger Danger! Stranger Danger! Stranger Danger!" the parents would yell, spluttering their lattes.

So I crawled into a bush. It soon became apparent that I wasn't the first one to have done this, because there were all sorts of objects there, ranging from the gross to the really gross. Ignoring them, I changed out of my Grammar uniform and into generic shorts and a generic T-shirt; I wanted to look as anonymous as possible. Removing myself from the bush and its crop of gross objects, I sat on a bench and took ClamTop out of my schoolbag.

"Open," I said, and it responded straightaway, opening.

Available Wi-Fi Networks, it said on the top of the screen.

GRAMMARNET was the one that interested me, so I double-tapped on the screen.

As I'd expected, it was a secure network. The password cracker immediately appeared, the little red devil doing its devilish dance, the words *cracking password* ... flashing underneath.

It took about fifteen seconds for it to start smiling, for the words *password cracked* to appear.

As you'd expect with such a big school, there were hundreds of computers connected to the network. They were arranged alphabetically, however, and it didn't take me long to scroll down and find Mr. Travers's computer. I could picture him sitting at his desk, reading out each student's name in his oxygen-depleting voice.

"Albrechtson?"

"Here, sir."

"Betts?"

"Here, sir."

When I brought up his desktop, I could see that Facebook was open. So that was why he was always bothering his computer. But I could also see that the Computerized Roll Call program was open and that he'd already put a digital tick against all the names except for mine. I touched the box next to my name and, hey presto, a tick appeared. I was just in time, too, because suddenly the "Send Data" button highlighted. The data downloaded to the main office would now show that, despite my empty seat, I was at school. Which meant that an automated text message – *Our records show that your son Dominic Silvagni is not attending school today. Could you please call immediately with an explanation* – would not be sent to both my dad's and my mum's phones. I packed up ClamTop, hoisted my bag over my shoulder and walked quickly away.

I reckon I've seen just about every James Bond film there is and I've never seen him pull out a Things To Do list.

The only stuff you saw him do was the crazy spectacular stuff – and occasionally the sexy stuff – but never the mundane stuff like shopping at Coles or getting his car serviced or getting angry because the gadget he bought on eBay looked nothing like it did in the photo.

But then again, he did have his support staff to do all that.

But I had no Mrs. Moneypenny. No Q. And I definitely wasn't licensed to kill.

I pulled a folded piece of notebook paper out of my pocket – my Things To Do list.

Uniform was the first thing.

I took out my phone and dialed a number.

"Hello, Big Pete's Pizzas. May I have your order please?"

She sounded Asian, but Asian-with-an-American-accent Asian.

"I didn't actually want to order a pizza," I said.

"We have a range of other non-pizza-based options on our menu, sir," she said. "And if gluten is a problem, then we have our new delicious non-gluten pizza crust."

"No, I didn't actually want to order anything, I just wanted to ask about your uniforms."

"Our uniforms?"

"That's right, like, we're having this thing at school," I said, thinking on my feet. "And I'm coming as a pizza delivery dude. So I wanted to see if I could buy one of your uniforms."

"Just hang on," the woman said, and then there were all sorts of noises.

"Excuse me, are you still there?" I said eventually.

Her Asian-but-American voice came back on the phone. "I just had to take off my shirt, to see the label, sir."

Now I felt like some sort of perve, the sort

that calls up pizza places and tricks the staff into removing their shirts.

"It's made by Acme Uniforms, sir," she said.

"Seriously? Acme? As in the Roadrunner?"

"That's what it says here, sir."

I thanked her profusely, googled "Acme Uniforms" on my iPhone, and hailed a taxi.

Acme Uniforms was easy to find; it was a large warehouse-type building, just off the Gold Coast Highway. What was difficult was finding a way to actually get into this large warehouse-type building.

Eventually I found it: an anonymous door at the back.

I pushed it open and it led into a small glass-partitioned office.

A woman, her piled-up hair held in place with what looked like chopsticks, was sitting at her desk, typing at an ancient computer, her back to me.

"How can I help you, darl?" she said, not looking up from the screen.

"I wanted to buy a Big Pete's Pizzas uniform," I said.

"Big Pete supplies his staff with their uniforms," she said, and then, with copious sarcasm: "Heart as big as a pumpkin, our Big Pete."

She still didn't look up. But then I realized that I could see the reflection of her face in one of the glass partitions. Which mean that she could, likewise, see my reflection.

The story about the thing at school, about coming as a pizza delivery dude, had worked with the woman on the phone – she'd taken off her shirt, hadn't she? – but somehow I didn't think it would do the trick here.

I had to come up with something else, something that made use of the fact that obviously this woman thought pumpkin-hearted Big Pete was a tightwad.

So I told her how my big brother worked for Big Pete's and how he'd spilled ink all over his uniform when he'd tried to help me refill the cartridge on my printer and how his uniform was now ruined and how if Big Pete found out for sure my big brother would get the sack and that would mean we wouldn't have the money to buy the medicine my sick mother so desperately needed.

The woman studied my reflection for what seemed like ages before she said, "What size is this brother of yours?"

"He's about my size, I guess," I said.

"Now why aren't I surprised?" The woman got up from her seat and she and her chopsticks disappeared through a door.

Was she going to get the manager? Or security? Or maybe even the tightwad himself, Big Pete.

But then there was a rustling sound and the woman returned holding a uniform wrapped in cellophane.

She threw it onto the counter.

"There you go," she said. "I figure anybody desperate enough to make up a story as ridiculous as that deserves to be rewarded."

"How much is it?" I asked.

The woman waved my question away. "Just don't rob any banks wearing it," she said, returning to her desk. "Or they'll have my guts for garters."

I grabbed the package, shoved it into my schoolbag and got out of there as quickly as I could before she changed her mind.

I took out the Things To Do list, the one that James Bond never used. The second item read: *more practice on mbike*.

Okay, I'd ridden a scooter up to the range and back, but that had been at a pretty sedate pace.

I wanted to practice some more, especially high-speed getaways.

I hailed another taxi to take me to an arcade in Surfers.

After handing a fifty-dollar bill to the excessively hairy man behind the counter, I said, "Two-dollar coins, please."

He held the bill up to the light, peering intently at it.

He must've seen the puzzled look on my face because he said, "You look like an honest type, but we've been getting a few shonky ones lately."

"Counterfeits?" I said.

"If you could call them that – most of them are just photocopies. Pathetic, the class of criminal you get these days."

I took the roll of coins he gave me and went over to the motorbike simulator.

I leaned this way and that way. I accelerated and I accelerated and I accelerated. And I started to get the hang of riding at high speed. In fact, on the very last coin I managed to come second to the great Valentino Rossi in the Italian Grand Prix.

As I walked out of the arcade, feeling quite pleased with myself, I heard the excessively hairy man say, "You've got to be kidding me!"

I looked around to see a scabby-looking kid standing at the counter while the man waved something in front of his face.

"Whatsamatta?" said the kid. "It's a fair-dinkum fifty."

"It's blank on one side, you idiot!" said the man as he leaned over and smacked the kid really, really hard across the ear.

The kid's head snapped to one side and he fell sprawling to the floor.

I realized then that it was Brandon, the kid from the hospital, the kid my mum knew.

For a second I thought about helping him but then decided against it – I had stuff to do.

Outside, I pulled out my piece of paper again.

Last thing on the list was *F of the E*.

Did I really need to go to Nimbin?

I mean, would James Bond go to Nimbin?

No, of course not. He'd go to Switzerland, or Tanzania, or Monaco, to somewhere more obviously cinematic.

But again, I wasn't James Bond. Not even close. I headed for Central Bus Station.

I'd met Zoe that day at the cafeteria, but I hadn't really been inside Central Bus Station before.

Why would I?

If my family needed to go anywhere we either drove or we flew. Long-distance buses were for, well, other people. And the concourse was full of those, well, other people getting off buses, getting on buses, waiting for buses. They were eating junk food out of Styrofoam containers. They were pulling overstuffed suitcases along on wonky wheels. They were stretched out on the floor, backpack for a pillow, sleeping in a fug of body odor. And there were continual announcements over the loudspeaker of bus arrivals and bus departures.

Yes, there was a lot to like about Central Bus Station.

And it occurred to me that if The Debt had done one thing, it had taken me to places I would never have gone to. Exciting places, cool places, like this.

"I'd like a round-trip ticket to Nimbin," I asked the man with the tongue stud behind the counter.

"Bus don't go to Nimbin," he said.

"It don't?" I said.

"No, not direct. You'd have to go to Byron and change there. But there's an hour wait."

The man must've seen the disappointment in my face because he said, "You could hitch?"

"Sorry?" I said.

"A lot of people get off on the Pacific Highway, at the turnoff. Then they stick out the thumb, eh? You'll always get a lift to Nimbin from there, it's that sort of place."

"Is it safe?" I said, and as soon as I did I wished I hadn't because I sounded like such a wuss.

"Well, I haven't heard of anybody getting knocked off," he said, and then he added, "not lately, anyway."

"Okay," I said. "I'll have a round-trip ticket to the turnoff."

"You're better off just buying a one-way," he said.

"Why's that?"

"Just in case you do get knocked off," he said, his face straight. "It'd be a waste of the return leg."

But then he broke into a smile.

"Mate, you should've seen the look on your face! Bloody priceless!" he said. "Look, you might get a lift all the way back to the Coast from Nimbin. Lots of people from here go there to buy their supplies, if you know what I mean. And if not, you can always buy a ticket from the driver on the bus itself."

I ended up taking his advice and buying a one-way ticket to the turnoff. I sat next to a Japanese backpacker who asked if he could practice his English on me.

I said, "Sure, as long as I can practice my jujitsu on you."

He didn't really get the joke, and after an hour it got pretty annoying having somebody practicing their English on you, so it was a relief when the bus pulled over onto the side of the road and the driver said, "Turnoff to Nimbin," and I could get off.

I stood under the sign that said *Nimbin 47 km* and stuck out my thumb and the very first car that came along, a Hilux pickup with a very excitable kelpie bouncing about in the back, stopped.

"Where you off to?" said the driver.

"Nimbin," I said, feeling every centimeter the professional hitchhiker.

"Well, my farm is only a few clicks up the road, but I guess every little bit counts," he said.

"Sure," I said, getting in.

Fifteen minutes later I was again standing on the side of the road with my thumb out, but this spot was much more isolated than the previous one. The thick rain forest on either side arched over the road, creating a canopy above me. And the air was heavy and host to a strange, unsettling assortment of rain forest sounds: clicks and grunts and croaks. I was starting to seriously question the macadamia farmer's every-little-bit-counts theory of hitchhiking.

Cars passed me, quite a few, until eventually one slowed down and a chubby-cheeked teenager with freckles and red hair leaned out of the window and said, "Do you want a lift, mate?"

"Sure," I said.

"Then drink a Red Bull!" he said, and the car roared off.

Idiot.

More cars passed and I was starting to think that I should find a way to get back to the Pacific Highway when an old Holden station wagon pulled up next to me.

Thank heavens, I thought.

"Where you off to?" said the man in the passenger seat.

He was in his thirties, maybe a bit older, and had a hard, mean face.

"Nimbin," I said.

"Well, you're in luck," said the man, his eyes flicking between me and my bag. "Hop in."

I moved closer to the car and opened the back door. I could see the driver now. His face was as soft as his passenger's face was hard, as friendly as his was mean.

"Too bloody hot to be standing out there," he said, smiling at me.

As I went to get in, I could smell stale cigarette smoke. I could smell stale sweat. And I could smell danger.

Whatever you do, don't get in this car, said one part of me.

But another part said, *You're a hitchhiker stuck in the middle of nowhere and this is what hitchhikers stuck in the middle of nowhere do, they get into strange cars.*

"Just move that stuff out of your way, if you like, matey," said the driver.

"You know what?" I said, closing the door. "I just changed my mind, so I reckon I might hitch back to Byron. But thanks heaps, anyway."

With that I hurried to the other side of the road, and thrust my thumb out, willing a car to appear.

The Holden station wagon stayed where it was and out of the corner of my eye I could see the driver watching me.

The rain forest was even noisier than before: more clicks, and more grunts, and more croaks. I wanted to be back in the Gold Coast, back in Halcyon Grove, within those enormous stone walls topped with razor wire. Yes, the men in balaclavas had found a way to get in, but Samsoni would never let two men like this come inside. Never. And even if he did, their every move would be tracked, displayed on a multitude of screens.

The station wagon inched forward, moved onto the road, and headed slowly towards Nimbin.

Thank heavens, I thought.

Then it turned around and accelerated straight towards me.

Competitive running is not just about running fast, it is also about making decisions under pressure: when to move, when to kick.

I figured I had about ten seconds until the station wagon was on me. One option was the rain forest, but I was worried that if I dived into it, it would be too thick; I wouldn't get very far. Another option was to play dodge. I was fast, with fast reflexes, surely I could keep out of the way of a sluggish old station wagon.

But as the station wagon got closer and I could see its occupants more clearly I realized that I was kidding myself, that I didn't have any options at all, because the passenger with the mean, hard face was holding a rifle.

Just as I was about to head for the rain forest I saw a car approaching from the other direction.

When the station wagon had almost reached me, I scampered across in front of it, stopping in the path of the other oncoming car.

It screeched to a stop.

I guess it didn't have much choice, it was either that or turn me into roadkill.

With a roar of its exhaust, the station wagon took off.

I explained to the driver, a dark-haired woman in her thirties, what had happened, amazed at how calm I felt. Yes, my heart rate was high, but it wasn't sky-high.

"You better get in," she said.

I hopped into the passenger's seat and she took off quickly.

"What is that boy doing in our car?" said a small girl from a booster seat in the back.

"We're just giving him a ride, Lauren," said the woman.

"I don't like him in here," said an even smaller girl from another booster seat next to Lauren's.

"Now, no need to be rude, Rosie," said the woman.

She wasn't actually headed to Nimbin – her daughters had swimming lessons in another town – but she said she'd take me all the way there anyway.

"How old are you?" she said.

"Sixteen," I replied.

"No, you're not," she said, studying my face.

"Okay, I'm fifteen, but I'm nearly sixteen."

"You're not running away from home, are you?"

"No," I said.

"And you're not scoring drugs or anything?"

Again, I told her no.

She seemed satisfied with this and didn't say anything for the rest of the trip, until she pulled up in the main street of Nimbin, outside the police station.

"So you're going to tell them exactly what happened?" she said.

"Sure."

"You okay for money?" she said, reaching for her purse.

"No, I'm fine," I said. "Thanks for the ride."

Just as I was about to close the door Rosie said, "Good-bye, you smelly boy."

I walked towards the police station, but when Lauren and Rosie and their car disappeared from sight, I turned and started walking down the main street. The Debt stipulated no police allowed. And even if I did report the two men in the station wagon, I doubted whether the police could've done much about it.

I mean, they hadn't actually done anything to me.

I continued walking down the street.

"Hey, you want some blow?"

"Hey, you want some Thai?"

"Hey, you want some E?"

By the time I reached the post office, I'd been offered six different types of drugs by four different people.

"No, thanks," I kept saying, but Nimbin was starting to unnerve me.

"Do you know where the Fiends of the Earth office is?" I asked a woman in a low-cut blouse and short skirt standing on the corner.

She looked at me with vampire eyes and said, "Yeah, but it'll cost you ten bucks."

"No, thanks," I said, walking quickly away.

Her voice followed me. "Down that street, take the second street on your left and there's a little mall about five minutes' walk, just past the Coast Home Loans."

I followed her directions, walked past the Hemp Embassy, and there was the office, across from the Mull Café.

I'd already decided against just barging in, figuring that covert surveillance was the way to go, so I ordered a Bengali chai at the café.

Remembering that James Bond never sat with his back to a door or a window, I chose a table where I had a good view of the Fiends of the Earth office, a wall plastered with posters behind me.

An hour and two Bengali chais later, the door to the office swung wide-open and a woman, who I assumed was the owner of the calm reasonable voice, came out.

She was in a wheelchair.

After locking the door, she took out her iPhone, starting doing stuff on it.

And immediately I could tell by the adoring look she was giving it, by the tender way she caressed the screen, that she, like my sister, was an iTragic.

After she'd finished she gave her iPhone one last lingering look before she put it away and wheeled down the mall and out of sight.

I guess it was possible that a woman in a wheelchair was capable of sinking a long-liner, of liberating twenty thousand chickens, of blowing up a whole lot of logging equipment.

It just didn't seem that possible, that's all.

I was just starting to think that I'd gotten this completely wrong, that I had come all this way, and drunk a whole lot of spicy tea, all for nothing, when the woman returned accompanied by two men.

Both men were tall, well built. Both men wore beards. But no shoes. Both men had dreadlocks. Though while they were waiting for the woman to unlock the office door I noticed that one of them had a large area on the back of his head that was dreadlock-free.

I took out my iPhone, switched to camera mode, zoomed in on this area. Just as I'd expected, it was a moonscape of scar tissue. I remembered what Dad had said that night: "Didn't one end up with third-degree burns to the dreadlocks?"

I reckoned I'd just found myself a couple of chicken-liberating, long-liner-sinking, logger-maiming ecoterrorists.

"You ready for another chai, luv?" asked the waitress.

"Do you have anything else to drink?"

"You've been drinking the Bengali, right?"

I nodded.

"Well, there's the Punjabi."

"Okay, I'll have one of those, thanks."

I sipped the Punjabi chai as slowly as possible

and there still hadn't been any action in the Fiends of the Earth office. I wondered whether now was the time to switch from covert to overt surveillance, whether I should go into the office and, under the guise of wanting some information about battery hens, check out what was happening in there.

In fact, I was just about to do this when the door opened and the woman wheeled out, accompanied by the two men. After locking the door, the three of them disappeared down the street.

No time to lose, I thought. If they'd gone to a late lunch, which I assumed they had, then I had thirty minutes, an hour at the most. I paid my bill and left.

Standing in front of the office, pretending to read the bulletin board, I took out my wallet, extracted my plastic Athletics Australia card, inserted it between the door and the doorjamb, and exerted pressure on it. There was a click and the door cracked open.

I slipped inside, locking the door behind me. There were posters of dead things on the walls: dead seals, dead whales, dead kangaroos. All in all, a pretty spooky sort of place, and now that I was here I realized that I didn't actually know why I was here, or what I was looking for.

I picked up a pamphlet from a table showing

photos of scrawny featherless chickens crammed into cages.

More spookiness.

But then I noticed something: the phone number at the bottom wasn't the number I'd called earlier.

In fact, it was a mobile number.

Was it hers? Scrawny featherless chickens crammed into cages did seem to be her specialty.

I shoved the pamphlet into my pocket.

There was only one door in this room. I opened it. It led to a bathroom. Well, half was the bathroom but the other half was being used as storage space. There were cardboard boxes, rolled-up banners, Grim Reaper masks, all sorts of weird activist stuff.

Then there were sounds: a door opening, muffled voices, footsteps.

They'd come back!

I dived into the pile of boxes, covering myself with a banner, making sure my bag wasn't showing.

The muffled voices became more distinct.

"So Mandy will pick us up at five, and then we'll go get the gear from the farmhouse."

"Seriously, Thor – Mandy?"

"She wants in, man."

Somebody entered the bathroom.

Through a chink in the cardboard I could see that it was the man with the moonscape head. Suddenly

I had a thought: *my phone's on!*

"I know, but …" he said, his voice trailing off.

The man undid his belt, dropped his shorts, sat on the toilet.

I moved my hand towards the pocket where my phone was, but as I did there was a rustle of paper so I stopped.

"You can't discriminate, man," said the other man. "If she wants in, she's in. And we know we can trust her."

"It's just that it's a tough gig, this one. That tower is, what, two hundred meters from the road. And that's rough country out there, Alpha."

So Thor was the one with the moonscape, Alpha was the one without.

"Chill, Thor. You heard what she said, she wants to drive, that's all."

"I'll have to clear it with the boss, anyway. He'll have final say," said Thor.

I recalled what I'd read about the Fiends of the Earth, their leader was a mysterious figure they liked to call Dr. E.

Thor grunted twice; there was a series of splashes and the room was instantly flooded with a horrendous suffocating smell.

Again I moved my hand towards my phone. Again there was a rustle of paper.

"Man, that's rotten, you been eating animal again?" said Alpha.

"Well, shut the door if it offends your delicate sensibilities," said Thor.

Alpha did just that.

The smell got exponentially worse, and seemed to be thicker, soupier.

I clamped one hand over my nostrils, but it seemed to enter my body from everywhere, through my ears, through my eyes, through my skin.

Why-o-why did Thor start eating animal again, why couldn't he have stuck to tofu and alfalfa sprouts?

Thor kept grunting, there were more splash sounds, and I thought I was going to faint. Finally there was the sound of paper being scrunched up, a toilet flushing, and I started to congratulate myself on my excellent undercover work.

And that was exactly when my phone went off.

As it did I automatically checked the caller ID. I mean, who would bother calling me during school hours?

Gus calling …

Blazing bells and buckets of blood!

179

SPEAKING IN TONGUES

I sat in a straight back chair, a light shining in my eyes, while the three of them grilled me.

"You can't keep me here," I said, going to stand up.

"Don't you bet on that," said Alpha, grabbing a handful of my T-shirt with his enormous paw and shoving me back into my seat.

I thought about the incident in North Queensland. Had they known that the logger was in the grader when they'd blown it up? I was starting to think that they had.

"Let's try this again," said Thor. "What are you doing here?"

"Like I told you, I was looking for money," I said.

Alpha had unzipped my bag and found the Big Pete's uniform in its plastic.

"What's this?" he said.

I shrugged.

He took out my school blazer.

"Grammar?" he said, looking at the insignia.

"Bulldust you were looking for money," said Mandy, her voice no longer so calm, so reasonable.

"Is Dr. Chakrabarty still there?" asked Thor.

"Yes," I said, wondering how he knew about Dr. Chakrabarty, the crusty old classics teacher.

"He must be at least a thousand years old by now," he said, and then I got it: Thor had gone to Grammar. Thor was an Old Boy!

"At least," I said.

"You called yesterday, didn't you?" said Mandy, moving her wheelchair closer.

"No," I said. "That wasn't me."

"More bulldust," she said, grabbing my iPhone.

After a couple of seconds she held up the iPhone to Thor. "See, he's lying, here's our number."

Thor now had ClamTop and was turning it around in his hands.

"What's this?" he said.

"What are you doing here?" said Mandy. "Who sent you?"

Too many questions; my head was starting to spin.

"Rough him up a bit," said Mandy to Alpha. "He'll talk then."

Alpha moved closer, drew his hand back – a huge hand that turned into a huge fist.

I cowered in the seat, covering my face with my arms.

"I really don't think that's the way we do things," I heard Thor say.

"Whack him!" said Mandy.

"He's a Grammar boy, not some street kid nobody cares about," said Thor. "You touch him and there'll be serious trouble."

"He's right," I said, looking through a crack in my fingers. "Serious trouble."

Alpha's fist morphed back into a hand and dropped to his side.

"Bulldust," said Mandy, and she ran over both my feet, my delicate runner's feet, with her wheelchair.

Small bones crunched and I screamed, "You freak!"

"Why, because I'm handi-capable?" said Mandy.

"No, because you ran over my feet, you freak!"

She went to run over them again, but I pulled my feet up.

"Okay," said Thor, putting ClamTop back into my bag. "You get out of here now."

"But –" started Mandy, before Alpha cut her off. "Thor's right, we have to let him go."

Which is what they did, but not before Mandy had removed all the money from my wallet.

"But that's stealing," I said.

"And you, Grammar Boy, were trespassing."

Outside, I hoisted my bag onto my shoulders and started walking. Not very well, because both feet were still throbbing with pain.

I wondered if Mandy had done them any permanent damage.

The door to Coast Home Loans opened and four men, all in suits, walked out towards me. They were deep in conversation, intent only on each other, and didn't notice me.

The man on the far left I knew pretty well: he was Rocco Taverniti. The man next to him I only knew from the news: he was Ron Gatto, our local state member, the one who had been elected after Imogen's father disappeared. The man next to Ron I didn't recognize but he was silver-haired, smooth-looking, older than the others. The man on the end I knew really well: he was my father.

"Dad!" I was about to say, but I quickly realized that probably wasn't the greatest idea, seeing as I was supposed to be at school, so I turned my back on them, pretending to be vitally interested in a brick wall.

Rocco Taverniti said something in a language I now knew to be Calabrian.

Why are you talking to my dad in Calabrian?

I wondered, remembering Dad's words from the other night: "I don't speakka the lingo."

But then Dad answered him in Calabrian. Surely I must be hearing things, I thought, looking up from the brick wall. But I wasn't. My father, his back to me now, was speaking fluent Calabrian.

The four men disappeared around the corner, and I had this urgent, almost overwhelming feeling that I needed to get out of this town. There was something not right about Nimbin, it was like a malevolent Wonderland, where hippies wanted to punch your lights out and your own father spoke in a strange tongue.

But how was I going to get home without any money?

I couldn't hitchhike. Not with the possibility that Dad would drive past. Not with the station wagon still out there.

I found the card in my wallet, dialed the number. He answered. "Luiz Antonio."

"Hi, it's Dom here. Look, I was wondering if you could pick me up again?"

"That's what us taxi drivers tend to do," he said.

Yes, yes, very humorous, Luiz Antonio.

"From where?" he asked.

"From Nimbin, just outside the post office."

A low whistle from the other end, followed by,

"You sure do get around, don't you?"

"Look, can you pick me up or not?" I said.

"I'll see you in ten minutes."

I was so happy to see Luiz Antonio's taxi, so glad to slide into the front seat, to be leaving Nimbin, that I didn't think about the ten minutes.

And all the way home I thought about other stuff.

Like Dad. How he was suddenly a stranger to me. The dad I knew, the dad I loved and who loved me, the dad I had known for my entire life only spoke one language: English. So who was this other Calabrian-speaking dad?

I thought about the Fiends of the Earth. If they were successful, then the lights might very well go out at 2000 hours. They probably wouldn't come back on at 2100 hours, though. Not with a tower down. That would take hours, even days, to fix.

I thought about how it wasn't just a matter of me putting my plan into action first, either. Because their reckless zealot of a plan was always going to gazump mine. I had to sabotage their plan before it sabotaged mine. But how? If I'd been a real terrorist, with a mandate from my god, then I could've taken the three of them out. If I'd been James Bond with a license to kill, then I could've done the same. But I wasn't. In fact, the idea of having to take anybody out, even somebody as obnoxious as Mandy, made

185

me feel a bit queasy. And the idea of returning to Nimbin made me feel even queasier.

But as we passed a shopping center, I had a thought.

"Do you mind pulling in there?" I asked Luiz.

"You're the customer," he said.

Once inside the center I did some quick googling on my iPhone, mentally adding several more entries to my list.

None of these would be difficult to find, but I knew from what other people had written on the net that it wasn't a good idea to try and buy them all in one place.

So I traipsed from shop to shop, until I'd acquired all the IED ingredients I needed, and then went back outside to where Luiz was waiting.

It was only much later, when I was in bed, that it occurred to me: what had Luiz Antonio been doing only ten minutes from the Nimbin Post Office?

The logical explanation was that he'd had a fare nearby, but how likely was that?

And what about when he picked me up from the Brisbane River?

He'd been following me.

But why?

And how?

DELIVERY BOY

Saturday, two hours before Earth Hour, and it couldn't have worked out better. In the morning Mom and Dad took their flight to Bali, for the renewal-of-the-renewal ceremony. They'd be back on Tuesday, in time for my race on Wednesday. In the meantime, Gus was looking after us.

As far as coaches went, Gus was a disciplinarian. As far as parental figures went, Gus was not. Which meant that Miranda and a whole lot of her nerd friends were up in her room listening to nerd music really loudly. Which meant that Toby was watching Jamie Oliver Uncut while systematically eating his way through the pantry. Which meant that when I told Gus I was going out he had two responses.

The first one was the non-disciplinarian grand-father's. "Okay, then."

The second one was the disciplinarian coach's. "Don't come back too late."

In my bedroom, I took one last look at Google Earth. I was just about to put ClamTop in my backpack when I stopped. Without ClamTop, without its awesome hacker power, my plan was rubbish, so I decided to make sure, for one last time, that it was working properly. I opened it. Immediately it went into Wi-Fi mode, displaying the local networks.

SILVAGNINET, HAVILLAND: they were all there.

Perfect.

But instead of closing ClamTop and packing it away, I kept staring at HAVILLAND, imagining Imogen sitting at her desk, hair cascading over her face, typing away at her computer.

I hacked into the network. Opened SYLVIA, Imogen's computer, and cloned her desktop. *This is crazy*, I told myself. *Earth Hour is less than two hours away and you're snooping around somebody's computer*. But I couldn't help myself. I went to Windows Mail. Went to "In-box." Scanned the messages.

guns&sixpack@hotmail.com. guns&sixpack@hotmail.com. And more guns&sixpack@hotmail.com!

I opened the latest message, sent an hour ago.

c u there when its dark!

My immediate thought was that I couldn't turn off the lights now, not if it meant that I would provide the darkness for Tristan and Imogen to get together. But I soon realized that was crazy.

I picked up my phone, tapped on Imogen's number.

"Don't," I was going to tell her.

Don't meet with Tristan. He doesn't really love you. He only wants one thing, and one thing only. Don't go. Don't. Don't. Don't!

But as soon as I heard Imogen's voice, as soon as she answered with, "Dom!" I knew I couldn't say it, because then for sure she'd know that I'd hacked into her computer.

"How did your petition go?" I said instead.

"They didn't even get back to me," she said. "Fascists."

I wanted to tell her that I was going to personally turn off the lights. And that it was me, not Tristan, who would do this for her.

But, again, I couldn't.

"Don't worry," I said. "The lights will go off."

Adopting an English accent, she said, "Is that you again, Harry Potter?"

"No, listen to me. The lights will go off. I promise you that."

"Okay, you're weird again."

"And Im?"

189

"Yes, Dom?"

Don't go near Tristan, I didn't say.

"I really like you, you know?"

"And I really like you," she said, "even though you've gone all weird on me."

"Actually, I probably love you," I said, except I hung up before I'd finished the sentence.

I put ClamTop in my backpack, made sure I had money in my wallet and called a cab.

"Will that be cash or charge?" the operator asked.

"Charge," I replied, giving her Dad's account name.

As soon as I'd done it, I realized how stupid it was – I'd just created a paper trail. And I'd seen enough TV cop shows to know not to leave clues like this.

I got the taxi to drop me off at the cinema and from there I walked back to Big Pete's Pizzas. I didn't go in, though. From the other side of the street I watched.

Watched the delivery boys, already wearing helmets, as they came out of Big Pete's Pizzas, carrying pizza boxes. Watched them load the boxes onto the backs of scooters. Watched them take off. Watched other scooters arriving. Watched as pizza delivery boys got off, not bothering to remove the keys. Watched as they hurried inside, still wearing their helmets.

I checked the time: it was almost seven. Time to stop watching. Time to start doing.

Moving further back into the shadows, I took off my sweater and tracksuit pants and stuffed them into my backpack under ClamTop.

Underneath I was wearing the blue-and-yellow of Big Pete's Pizzas.

I put on the motorbike helmet. Now I was sure I looked like any other Big Pete's Pizzas delivery boy, except for one thing: my size. Yes, I was a fairly big fifteen year old, but a fairly big fifteen year old does not an eighteen year old make. There wasn't much I could do about that, however.

I put the backpack on and crossed the street. It would've been easy just to get on a scooter and take off. But there was one thing missing: a pizza. And if you're going to impersonate a pizza delivery boy you better have some product to deliver.

I followed another boy inside. There was a row of seats, the first three of which were occupied by delivery boys. The boy I followed took the next available seat, and I took the one after.

"Halcyon Grove delivery," came a voice over the loudspeaker.

The boy in the first seat groaned.

"No tips, for sure," said the second boy. "Anybody want this?"

"No way," said the third boy.

"Not me," said the fourth boy.

"I've got it," I said, attempting to drop my voice a couple of octaves.

"It's all yours, Squeaky," said the first boy.

I got up and walked into the next room, to where two pizza boxes were sitting on the counter. I grabbed them, turned and started walking out when a voice said, "Hey, you!"

I looked around.

The voice belonged to Bryce Snell. This kid who used to go to my primary school. This bully who used to go to my primary school. One of the reasons I started running in the first place was to get away from Bryce Snell and his Chinese burns.

"Yes?" I said.

I was sure I'd been found out, my plan destroyed before it even had a chance to get going.

"You've forgotten the docket, dingbat."

I took the docket from Bryce Snell and got out of there.

I loaded the pizza boxes onto the nearest scooter and hopped on.

I turned the ignition key – the motor started. I twisted the throttle.

The scooter moved off, this time with no wobble.

Again, it felt pretty weird to be fifteen years

old and driving a scooter on the main road, in the middle of traffic. But I have to admit, it felt cool too. Criminal cool.

I drove through Surfers Paradise, through the blaze of lights. I checked my watch. An hour and fifteen minutes until Earth Hour. The car behind me beeped its horn.

Rack off, I thought.

Another beep. I looked around. It was a police car. I didn't feel so criminal cool now. The policewoman behind the wheel was making an opening and closing gesture with her hand.

What did she mean?

I considered a getaway, a high-speed chase through the city. But when I played that scenario out in my head, it ended with a crash, a broken scooter, a mangled kid and some very messy pizza.

Again, I looked around. The same gesture, hand opening and closing. But this time I got it: it was a blinking gesture. I'd forgotten to turn my lights on!

I switched them on. The policewoman smiled at me and I gave her a thumbs-up.

At the next lights I turned left off the main road, following the route I'd memorized from Google Earth. From here I took back roads, quiet residential streets, until I reached the entry ramp to the freeway. I hesitated – it looked way scary out there.

But I had no choice; there wasn't really any other way to get to Diablo Bay.

I rolled down the entry ramp, onto the freeway and into the insanity that was Saturday traffic.

Engines and exhausts, hissing air brakes, honking horns, all competing to make the most horrendous noise, a sort of Freeway Idol. And the air was toxic with fumes, like a chem lab gone feral.

Terrified, I kept to the edge of the road, following the white line. The cars, the trucks, the buses ripped past, not bothering to change lanes, and I was buffeted this way and that by their slipstreams.

For some reason I thought of another of Coach Sheeds's quotes, this one from the Finnish runner Paavo Nurmi. "Mind is everything. Muscle – pieces of rubber. All that I am, I am because of my mind."

Okay, I said to myself, *you might be only a fifteen-year-old kid on an 80 cc pizza delivery scooter, but you need to think like a truck.*

You're a Mack, a Kenworth, I said as, big wheels rolling, I moved further out onto the road.

It worked: the other vehicles shifted into the adjacent lane to pass now.

Diablo Bay Exit 2 km, said the sign ahead.

A beat-up car was now alongside me. The window wound down, revealing the Red Bull idiot.

No, it can't be. It's too much of a coincidence. But

it was him, alright. With his hideously chubby cheeks, and his hideously freckly freckles, and his hideously red hair.

"Is that the Supreme with extra anchovies we ordered?" he said.

I nodded, happy to go along with his excellent joke.

Diablo Bay Exit 1 km, said the sign ahead.

"You want some Coke to go with that?" he said.

I didn't get it – as a representative of a pizza retail organization it was my role to inquire as to my customer's beverage requirements.

Red Bull's arm, clutching a Coke bottle, extended out of the window. The bottle tilted, the liquid flying out.

Now I got it.

Coke sloshed over me. Into my helmet. Into my eyes.

I couldn't see.

I took my hand off the throttle to wipe the Coke out of my eyes. The scooter slowed.

From behind, the honk of a horn.

A truck was bearing down on me.

Hand back on the throttle, I twisted it hard.

The scooter surged, the honk stopped.

I could see again, but the Diablo Bay exit was behind me now.

I pulled onto the shoulder to consider my options.

The truck thundered past.

I could've taken the next exit, done a loop, but I didn't have a clue how far that was, how long it would take.

I didn't see that I had a choice, really. I bumped the scooter around until it was directly facing the traffic. And I took off, staying on the shoulder, keeping as far as possible to the right.

No longer was I a Mack, a Kenworth; no, I was a tiny little kid on a tiny little scooter.

The cars that were coming at me, with their lights and their grilles, looked like predators, like huge metal sharks.

And I couldn't help thinking that any second I was going to hear the sound of a police siren. Or that a helicopter would suddenly appear overhead, rotors carving the air, just like in the movies.

But eventually I reached the exit and I was able to get off the freeway and away from the ravenous sharks.

AIN'T NO TOWELHEAD

As I neared the checkpoint I slowed down. Not completely, though. I was hoping that the guard would see I was a harmless pizza delivery boy and not some crazed bomb-toting terrorist, and wave me through. The boom gate remained lowered, however, and I was forced to come to a somewhat shaky stop. A powerful spotlight shone directly into my eyes.

Sitting there I felt so exposed, almost naked.

Eventually a door opened and a guard approached. Because of the light in my eyes I couldn't see him properly. I'd already considered the possibility that I would run into Buzz Lightyear, but I'd decided that the chances of that were very small, that it was an acceptable risk. For a start, the station must've employed hundreds of guards. And it was a different day of the week than the excursion. A different time of day.

The guard stepped in front of the light. I could see his face now. And it was him, the acceptable risk, Woody's buddy, Buzz Lightyear.

Right then I hated Kenny McCann.

Why did he make that pathetic joke?

Why did I laugh at his pathetic joke?

"You new or something, pizza boy?" said Buzz.

I wasn't sure how to answer this; was it some sort of trick question?

In the end I said, "Yes, sir."

And I immediately regretted the "sir" – this was a security guard, not a knight of the realm.

"And they didn't tell you?" he said.

"No, sir," I said, having figured that now I'd started with the "sir" thing, I'd better keep it up. "Tell me what, sir?"

"To take your rutting helmet off, pizza boy. So we can see you ain't no towelhead."

Right then, I knew I was a goner.

If I removed my rutting helmet, he would surely recognize me as the kid on the bus; he'd taken a photo of me, after all.

What other options did I have?

I could tell him that I'd forgotten the complimentary garlic bread and turn around and make a run for it. But then Buzz would probably assume that I was indeed a towelhead and that he was within his rights – in fact he'd be doing a service to his country – to pull out his gun and plug me several times in the back.

I slid off my helmet.

Buzz, a halo of light around his head, looked straight at me. His brow furrowed.

"Don't I know you from somewhere?" he said.

"I get around a bit," I said.

More brow. More furrow.

Until Buzz said, "What sort of pizza is it?"

"I don't make 'em, I deliver 'em," I said, figuring it was about time I went on the offensive. "And if I don't get going soon, somebody, probably your boss, is going to be eating cold pizza."

"Okay, then," said Buzz with a wave of his meaty hand. "But remember next time, rutting helmet off."

I slid my helmet back on, twisted the accelerator, took my feet off the ground and wobbled off towards the plant.

I checked the time: 7:45.

I was behind schedule, so I twisted the throttle harder; the scooter responded and we flew down the road.

I could see the plant ahead, lit up like a carnival, plumes of dusky smoke rising upwards, disappearing into the starless sky. I was definitely within range now, but because there were high cyclone fences on both sides of the road there was nowhere to pull over. I kept going, stopping when I reached the well-lit parking lot. There were twenty or so parked cars, but no people.

A quick glance at the building confirmed my suspicions: CCTV cameras and plenty of them. Already I was on a screen, probably more than one. Soon to be on a file, on a hard disk. And tonight, no doubt, I'd be backed up, duplicated, taken off-site.

I parked next to a Toyota Land Cruiser.

As I went to remove the pizza boxes I noticed for the first time the name on the docket – Silvagni.

For a second I was completely freaked out, until I realized what had happened: Miranda and her nerd friends must've ordered pizzas and I just happened to have picked them up. Or maybe it was Toby: having polished off the pantry, he'd started feeling a bit hungry again.

Still with my helmet on, I walked towards the door. With each step I expected a voice to boom over a loudspeaker: "Remove the helmet! Remove the helmet now!"

The problem was, if I removed my helmet, then the person reduplicated on the hard disk was no longer just a generic pizza delivery boy, he was

Dominic Silvagni, Enemy of the State.

When I got close enough to the wall I took a couple of quick steps and flattened myself against it. From there I could no longer see the CCTV cameras. I figured if I couldn't see them, they couldn't see me. I shuffled along the wall, moving away from the door, until I got to the corner of the building. I ducked around, shuffling along the wall for ten or so meters. Although it was much darker here, and I couldn't see any cameras, I still felt exposed. But a glance at my watch showed that I didn't have time to look for somewhere more secluded. I dumped the pizza boxes, took off my backpack and removed ClamTop.

"Open!" I said.

It opened, immediately displaying the available wireless networks.

There was only one: DIABLONET. I double-tapped on this.

A box popped up, asking for a password. As before, ClamTop's password cracker immediately went into action, the little red devil dancing his devilish jig.

This time it took much longer, maybe even a minute, for it to crack the password. When it had, the screen was divided into a series of smaller boxes. In such a big organization you would expect a complex network with many computers connected to it. But the sight of so many of them – there must've been at least a hundred! – unnerved me, panicked me. All those boxes. All those words. Soon they were going to start squirming like worms.

This is too much.

I can't do this.

"Form is everything," Gus always says. "The bedrock. When all else fails, find your form."

I tried to find my form: I forced my shoulders down from where they were hunched around my ears; I breathed in deeply, from the diaphragm. I returned my attention to the screen, to the first box in the top row. It was called React01.

That's not what you're after, I told myself.

The next box was called React02.

That's not what you're after, either.

From there I kept going systematically, from box to box, until halfway along the fifth row I came across three boxes that were called Transf01 Transf02 Transf03.

Transf for Transformer, I thought.

I selected these three boxes.

There were now three cloned desktops, side by side, on my screen. Immediately I could see that they were running Windows 7, which was a relief, because I'd half expected the plant to use Linux, or some even more exotic operating system.

On the middle one somebody was writing an email in Windows Mail.

I could meet you outside cinema at 9, they typed.

Again, I experienced that feeling I'd had when I'd cloned Imogen's desktop – that I was trespassing on somebody's private life, that I was somewhere I had no right to be.

It didn't last very long, though.

I maximized that screen.

I already knew that what I did on the cloned desktop was not reflected in the original. So I minimized Windows Mail.

There were a number of digital meters on the desktop.

Reactor Output.

Transformer Input.

Transformer Output.

All these made sense to me, but they weren't what I was looking for.

Gabriel's words came back to me: "There's an operator override on everything."

That was what I was looking for.

I scanned the desktop icons, searched through the drop-down menus, but I couldn't see anything that resembled an operator override function. I wondered whether I had this completely wrong, whether the override was something that had to be given verbally, by telephone.

But again I recalled Gabriel's words. "I input them here and they get shunted up to the plant."

But maybe Gabriel had been trying to make himself appear more important than he actually was. He hadn't seemed that sort of person, though.

I went back through the icons, back through the drop-down menus. Again there was nothing that resembled an operator override function. But then I remembered that Windows 7 had a "Search Programs and Files" feature. I typed *operator override* into that, hit return. It took three seconds to find it, a hidden icon. I double-tapped on that and a screen popped up, with three entry fields.

Reactor Production Amount, said the first.

I entered *0* into that box.

Start Time, said the second.

I entered *2030.*

Finish Time, said the third.

As I entered *2130,* I was suddenly bathed in harsh light.

Caught!

Caught hacking into the network of a nuclear power station.

I hadn't given too much thought to what would

be the consequences if this happened.

It had seemed unduly pessimistic. I'd been in total bulletproof mode: me, caught? No way!

But now that I had been caught, I did a lot of thinking really quickly. I would be tried under the new antiterrorism laws. Sent to jail forever. And even my father, with all his money, wouldn't be able to get me out. They'd ask me why I did it, who I was working for. Because of The Debt, because of the *Omertà*, I wouldn't be able to tell them. So they'd resort to torture. Not in Australia, of course, because torture is illegal here. So they'd fly me offshore, maybe even to Guantanamo Bay. They'd play Céline Dion records at earsplitting volume, all day and all night. They'd waterboard me. Until, eventually, I'd be reduced to a dribbling idiot. Losing a leg to The Debt didn't seem so bad anymore. The lesser of two atrocities.

Then there was the sound of a car accelerating, and the light disappeared, and I was back in semi-darkness. It had only been a car swinging out of the parking lot.

I moved the cursor into the "Send" box. Checked the figures again before I tapped on the screen.

Immediately a pop-up appeared.

Password.

No problem, I thought; my little mate the devil

could crack any password. And just as I expected, he soon appeared, clutching his trident, and started cracking, dancing his devilish jig.

After twenty or so seconds there was no triumphant smile, however. Instead, a message appeared: *Cracker has detected md5-crypt with a 24-bit salt encryption. Brute Force may take up to 24 hours. Please provide precomputation string.*

Fortunately I'd done enough reading to understand this – when people set a password, they usually don't use random letters and numbers, they include a word that has particular relevance to them: a precomputation string.

I started with the obvious, typing *Gabriel* into the box.

More dancing, but again that message appeared. I tried *Gabby* but with the same result.

What else did I know about Gabriel?

Again I went back to our excursion, replayed the video of our visit to ze transformer in the YouTube of my mind.

"Tomorrow night the Mariners are playing the mighty Tritons," Gabriel had said.

Why did he say the mighty Tritons, not just the Tritons? Because he rooted for them, that was why.

I typed in *Tritons*.

No luck.

What did I know about the Tritons?

Not much, because I wasn't that interested in soccer, or football, or whatever they called it. But then I remembered the photo of Rocco Taverniti I'd seen on the net.

He'd had his arm around the star recruit, a Brazilian.

What was his name again?

Zongaga?

Gonzaga, that was it!

I typed in *Gonzaga*.

Five seconds later the devil was grinning and so was I. The password may have used md5-crypt with a 24-bit salt encryption, but it'd cracked it like a walnut.

Another pop-up appeared: *Message Received by Reactor*.

I closed ClamTop, put it back into the backpack, and put the backpack on my back.

I went to step over the dumped pizza boxes, but stopped. Suddenly, I felt ravenously hungry. And everybody agreed: Big Pete's Pizzas were the best pizzas in town. It would be a shame to waste it all. Especially since it was my sister – or maybe even my brother – who'd ordered it. I opened a box, removed a slice. Cramming it into my mouth, I moved to the edge of the building.

A quick glance – there was nobody there. I repeated the back-flat-against-the-wall maneuver, this time moving towards the door. When I'd reached the right place I moved quickly away from the wall and towards my scooter. As I did I could feel the CCTV camera on me, tracking me, storing multiple versions of me on the hard disk.

When I reached my scooter, a car started up. Perfect, I told myself. Buzz may have been stupid, but he wasn't that stupid. I was sure he was keen to ask me a few questions on my way out, like why it had taken me eleven minutes to deliver a pizza. I needed to find another way to exit, one that didn't necessarily involve Buzz.

I started the scooter up and waited. When a car moved past, I swung in behind it, following its red taillights as it moved down the road.

Not too close! I warned myself. I didn't want the driver to get suspicious.

But when I saw the glow of the checkpoint I accelerated, moving closer. The car ahead slowed down and the boom gate swung up. I twisted the throttle hard. The scooter was no racing machine: it took a while to respond. The car passed through and the boom gate was already on its way down when I got there. I flattened myself along the scooter, my nose pressing against the speedometer.

The boom gate came down, karate chopping me across the back of the neck. The pain was sharp and intense and the force knocked the scooter off-kilter so that it skittered across the road. I put out a foot and pushed hard against the road surface.

It worked: the scooter righted itself.

I held my breath. Surely a siren would sound any second now. But it didn't; nothing disturbed the night's stillness except the sound of my exhaust.

I allowed myself a peek over my shoulder.

A silhouetted security guard, square shoulders, even squarer jaw, standing outside, his back to the boom gate, zipping up his fly.

Buzz, you're lucky I'm not a certain Mr. bin Laden back from the dead, because if I was, you'd be kebab right now.

THE DODDLE

Really, it should have been a doddle from there. Enjoy the ride home, get rid of the scooter, then hang around the city until Earth Hour started. Maybe even grab a bite to eat, have a look around the amazing new Styxx technology store that had just opened up at Surfers ... Except for one thing, or three things: the Fiends of the Earth.

When I came to the old tomato stall, where the road passed close to the transmission tower, I pulled over.

As I wheeled the scooter behind the stall, I remembered what Seb had said on the day of the excursion. "Imagine if that tower fell down."

Yes, Seb, imagine if it did.

The Earth Hour people had chosen the ideal night: there was little moon, only a few stars, so it was quite dark, and I could only just make out the hulking shape of the transmission tower in the distance.

This was both a good thing – I'd be more difficult to spot – and a bad thing: it wouldn't be easy traversing the terrain.

Thor was right, it was rough country out here.

I took out my iPhone, started up the iTrack app.

Of course, there was a possibility that she wouldn't bring her iPhone, that she would leave it at home, but I figured it wasn't much of a possibility.

I'd seen the adoration in her eyes, I'd noted the tender way she caressed the screen – Mandy had a very bad case of iLove, a case that made my sister's iLove look pretty anemic.

I entered Mandy's number, the one from the flyer, and just as it had done last night when I'd tested it, the iTrack app did some thinking before it spat out a GPS position. I touched this and it took me to Google Maps.

Mandy and her iPhone were on this very road, about 5.3 km away!

I waited a few minutes and repeated the process.

They were now 5.1 km away and headed in my direction. And, according to iTrack, they were moving at 64.8 kph.

There would be no doddle, no bite to eat, no leisurely perusal of the Styxx store and its wares; it was time to put Plan Moneypenny into action.

211

I made my way quickly towards the tower, pack jogging against my back, stumbling a couple of times on rocks.

When I reached the tower I took off my backpack and carefully removed the IED from inside.

As I did, I had this sudden feeling of ... I'm not sure what you would call it. Power? Satisfaction? Maybe even arrogance?

I, Dominic Silvagni, fifteen years old, of Halcyon Grove, had, with my very own hands, made this smooth, round device packed with malice and destruction.

I gaffer-taped it to a leg of the tower, making sure that the fuse was easily accessible. Then I took out my iPhone to check iTrack, but I needn't have bothered, because I could already see the sweep of approaching headlights.

A van appeared, the shape of a collapsible wheelchair visible on the top. It passed, and my whole meticulously worked out plan was instantly worthless. Then it appeared again, coming from the opposite direction, pulling up just beyond the tomato stall.

I watched as two men got out – Thor and Alpha – dressed in black, black smeared on their faces, both of them barefoot. They took packs out of the back and started towards the tower, moving stealthily, almost gliding over the ground.

Any doubt I might have harbored about their capabilities instantly disappeared. These were eco-ninjas, and they were capable of anything, of liberating all the KFC-bound chickens in Australia, of sinking a hundred long-liners, of blowing up every piece of logging equipment in every old-growth forest in the world.

And suddenly I felt angry, angry that The Debt had cast these two as my enemies.

Because, in a way, I admired them.

And now I had to take them out.

As they approached, gliding across the ground, I got ready.

This part of Plan Moneypenny had always been the most unsatisfactory. If I'd been Taliban, or an Iraqi insurgent, or a professional fighter, the son of a professional fighter, himself the son of a professional fighter, possessed of all that accumulated knowledge, I was sure I'd be standing behind the tomato stall, mobile phone in my hand, ready to remotely detonate my IED.

One press of the hash button and *kaboom!*

But I wasn't, and I hadn't been able to work out how to do it, so here I was, lighter in my hand, about as non-remote as you could get.

I waited a couple more seconds until I could make out the eco-ninjas' faces, before I told myself *Now!* and lit the fuse.

It glowed red but it didn't take, and for a second I thought I'd been had, that what I'd seen a hundred times on YouTube had been some sort of practical joke. But then there was a loud fizzing sound – the fuse had taken! – and I had to get out of there.

This next part of Plan Moneypenny really depended on one thing and one thing only: leg speed, on me getting to my scooter as quickly as possible.

Being a runner, I thought I had that covered.

But now I wasn't so confident; even walking here, watching my every step, I'd stumbled twice.

I took off.

Not in a straight line, because I didn't want to pass the eco-ninjas coming the other way.

So I ran in a sort of arc, cross-country technique: toes pointed, legs pumping high, arms swinging hard.

Miraculously I dodged the rocks and managed to stay upright.

When I reached the road, I realized my arc had brought me really close to the Fiends of the Earth van.

I wasn't too worried, though: Mandy was in a wheelchair, what could she do?

Well, she could turn the headlights on high beam.

Which was exactly what she did.

Dazzling the crap out of me.

She could lean on her horn.

Which was exactly what she did.

Scaring the crap out of me.

And she could try to run me over.

Which, again, was exactly what she did.

Revving the engine, she dropped the clutch. The handi-capable freak!

And dazzled, scared as I was, I just stood there as the van, gathering momentum, came onto me.

From the direction of the transmission tower came a sound, more than just a sound, a mega-sound, an almighty *kaboom!* Which was enough to shock me into action.

I leapt to one side, and the van, lights still dazzling, horn still blaring, thundered past.

A couple of commando-style rolls and I was back on my feet.

The transmission tower was now incandescent, an enormous roman candle, sparks showering skyward.

For a second I thought I'd overdone it, that I'd actually taken the tower out, but I had to remind myself that my IED wasn't really an IED. Yes, it was definitely I for improvised, and it was definitely D for a device, but it wasn't E for explosive, it was just a whole bunch of sparklers bought at different shops bound closely together with layers of electrical tape. Really, it was just an ID.

Just as I reached my scooter the sirens started.

GETTING OFF EVEREST

It's not getting to the top of Mount Everest that kills people, it's getting off it. So what's my point? Exactly that. I'd climbed Everest – sort of – and now I had to get off it.

I'd spent hours and hours in front of my computer, zooming in and out of Google Earth, planning an escape route, memorizing the safest way off Everest. It'd seemed straightforward then, but now that it was dark, with sirens blaring from all directions, it didn't seem so simple.

Stick to the plan! I kept telling myself, especially the part of me that just wanted to keep going flat out on the road I was on.

I passed over the bridge, and there it was: a dirt road leading off to the right. I took it, turning off my lights as I did. I had to slow right down but at least

I was moving away from the main road. The sirens were less audible here, and I was getting more confident that I'd made my escape.

I approached another bridge, but it wasn't there!

I remembered it clearly from Google Earth: a normal, everyday bridge, nothing fancy, nothing ornate. But it had done – in Google Earth, anyway – exactly what bridges were supposed to do: take the road from one side of the river to the other.

Instead, there were piles of sand and piles of gravel and huge concrete blocks and earthmoving machines and a sign that said *We're Building You a Better Gold Coast! Please Use Detour.*

Right then, I hated Google Earth, hated Google anything. But I had no choice, so I took the detour. I knew exactly where it was taking me. I knew because I'd done everything I could to avoid this route.

I could smell it even before I got there.

The smell of finite existence.

And when I did get there, to the stone wall, to the looming shapes beyond, I forced myself to look the other way. There were two kilometers of Necropolis to get past, two kilometers of galloping coimetrophobia to deal with.

I heard them first – a distant *thwocka thwocka thwocka* – before I saw their sweeping searchlights.

Helicopters!

I was so angry with myself: I'd seen enough action movies, why hadn't I factored in helicopters?

The anger quickly became concern, because they were approaching rapidly. I needed to find cover. To my right there was nothing but open fields. I forced myself to look left. At the unbroken stone wall. I almost felt relief: there was no way in anyway.

Thwocka! Thwocka! Thwocka!

Suddenly, an entrance. I slowed down, wheeled over to the gate. Pushed against it.

Surely it would be locked, I thought. I hoped.

It wasn't.

Thwocka! Thwocka! Thwocka!

I was inside the Necropolis.

"Hey, did any of you guys here order pizza?" I said.

Nobody laughed.

Not even me.

I rolled down a path, on either side of which were row upon row of gravestones.

No cover there.

Thwocka! Thwocka! Thwocka!

The helicopters and their sweeping searchlights were getting closer.

I kept going, looking for somewhere to hide.

But when I found it, I wish I hadn't.

It was the Tabori family crypt.

There were Taboris at my school, twins. One played cello, the other violin in the school orchestra.

As I pushed against the door with the front wheel of my scooter I wondered if this was their family crypt, whether one day, after the final note had sounded, they would both end up here. The door creaked inwards, and my scooter and I disappeared inside.

If you wanted to destroy somebody who has arachnophobia, what would you do?

Stick them in a cage full of spiders.

Somebody who has altophobia?

Stick them on the top of Everest.

Somebody who has coimetrophobia?

Do this to them. Stick them in a crypt at night.

The pressure was intolerable – it was building in my head, my whole body. I had to get out of here.

I tried to reason with myself. What was coimetrophobia, after all? It was just a word some mint-sucking psychiatrist had written on a piece of paper with an expensive fountain pen, that's all it was.

But there was no reasoning. The pressure was increasing, the terror was increasing. Every fiber, every atom in me was screaming: *get us out of here!*

The *thwocka thwocka thwocka* was overhead, however. I could almost feel the whirring rotors as they shredded the night sky.

Harsh light entered through a high-set window, illuminating the inside of the crypt. There were plaques on one wall, with photos of the residents, the deceased. One of the faces was familiar, somehow. Who was it? Then it came to me: it was one of the twin boys in the photo I'd found in the bottom drawer of Gus's desk.

It's the coimetrophobia, I told myself. *It's playing tricks with your mind.*

Then I saw the rat.

Miranda used to have a rat called Madonna that had pink eyes and white fur and would only eat unsalted cashew nuts. This rat had black fur and black eyes and was looking straight at me, a quizzical look on its rat face, like it'd never seen a human before. And maybe it hadn't. Not a vertical one, anyway.

The light disappeared and the rat was sucked back up by the darkness.

The *thwocka thwocka thwocka* moved away.

I knew I had to stay here, that the helicopters were probably following some sophisticated searching algorithm that would bring them sweeping over the same place several times. But I couldn't.

Coimetrophobia was not just a word written on a piece of paper.

I backed the scooter out of there, and then I took off, flying down the path, through the gate and back onto the road.

Fortunately, the helicopters didn't return and I was able to finish the detour and get back to my planned escape route, a series of small tracks that went this way and that, past farmhouses and milking sheds.

When I'd reached the main road again, I pulled over into a stand of trees. I changed back into my clothes, shoving the delivery boy's uniform into a plastic bag.

My instinct was to rid myself of the bag there and then by burying it under some rocks, or by climbing up a tree and wedging it between some branches. But I'd already been through this in my head. If I did this, it would still be evidence, evidence rich in DNA, evidence that somebody, someday, might find. No, I had to take the uniform with me.

I took the can of black spray paint and gave the scooter a quick and dirty spray job, obliterating any mention of Big Pete's Pizzas. I did the same with my helmet. Satisfied that I looked a lot less like a pizza delivery boy that maybe had an alert out on him, I got back on the scooter.

I imagined I could hear the freeway's roar now. Almost see it, the river of noise and light. Freedom, I thought, because surely once I got on there, I would be anonymous again.

Headlights appeared from towards Diablo Bay, and then a van moved slowly past. Strapped to its roof rack was a collapsible wheelchair.

They'd gotten away!

Not possible, I thought. Because I was sure I'd brought a world of trouble down on them, a world of roadblocks and buzzing helicopters and trigger-happy antiterrorist squads. Still, now that they had managed to get away, I figured it was better just to let them go. There was no way the reckless zealots were going to bring that tower down now.

But then I thought of Mandy.

The way she'd run over my feet, my delicate runner's feet, in her wheelchair. The way she'd almost run over all of me, the delicate all of me, in her van.

Not only that, it seemed like I hadn't finished the job. That I wasn't doing Plan Moneypenny the justice that it – she? – deserved.

So, killing my lights, I took off after them.

Fortunately for me they weren't going very fast, obviously going for the we're-not-running-from-anything look, the we're-just-on-a-drive-in-the-country-at-night look. So it didn't take me long to catch up with them and as I did I worked out a plan, my third one for the night.

Now I had a problem, however; a classic catch-22. In order to execute the plan, I needed to pass them, but if I passed them they'd immediately be onto me.

But as soon as this catch-22 appeared, so did its solution.

Rest Stop Ahead said the sign, and I remembered how on the day of the excursion we'd pulled in here so all my over-caffeinated classmates could relieve themselves.

The van continued straight ahead, and I veered to the left, onto the gravel road.

As I did I twisted the throttle as far as it would go.

Okay, there was no way this scooter would have come second to the great Valentino Rossi in the Italian Grand Prix. The great Valentino Rossi probably wouldn't even want his Ham and Pineapple delivered by such a thing. But it was surprisingly powerful, and as it flew across the loose gravel, both my hands and thighs gripping tightly, I had the sensation that I was no longer in control.

That I was being hurtled forward by forces far greater than me.

And all I could do was what I was already doing: hold on tightly.

And maybe it would all end then; the tires would lose traction and the bike would slide out from under me and we'd both smash into a tree. Or maybe not.

Suddenly the gravel road ended and I was back on the main road.

I glanced over my shoulder, to see the twinkle of headlights far behind me.

I'd done it.

I kept the throttle at maximum until I came to the place where the bus had stopped for the cows that day.

I pulled the scooter off the road, killed the engine.

I couldn't see them but now I could hear them: moos, moos and more moos. They sounded quite agitated and I couldn't blame them. All those blaring sirens, all those thwocking helicopters, would've stirred up anybody.

I hurried towards them. Now I could smell them, and their poo, feel the warm fug of their collective breath.

"Hello, girls," I said, opening the gate. "Time to get a move on."

They stayed where they were.

"Come on!"

No movement.

I ran across the road and pushed the other gate open. There was a loud creaking sound. Almost immediately, the cows started moving across the road towards me.

I let a couple through the gate, but then I did a very mean thing: I closed the gate. Then I ran across the road and did another very mean thing: I closed the other gate.

There were now at least thirty cows on the road: a bovine roadblock.

I found a good hiding place behind a tree.

Lights went on in the farmhouse. And headlights appeared on the road.

The van arrived first.

Perhaps another type of terrorist, a member of the Taliban, for example, might have just barreled through, knocking cows helter-skelter like bowling pins. Not the chicken-liberators, however.

They stopped, they dimmed their lights, and Thor leaned out of the window and said, "Let's work through this, people."

There was the click of a flashlight and the dairy farmers arrived.

They were both short and round, both wearing bathrobes and gum boots, and one of them was carrying a double-barrel shotgun.

"What the blazes is going on here?" she said, pointing it straight at Thor.

"I reckon we might have just caught ourselves some terrorists, Ducks," said the other dairy farmer, taking out a phone. "Might just give that number they gave us a call."

"Ladies, you've got this wrong," said Thor.

"For a start, we're no ladies," said the dairy farmer called Ducks. "And secondly, let us be the ones to decide if we've got it wrong or not."

"Yes, that's right," said the other dairy farmer to whoever was on the other end of the phone. "We'll be waiting for you."

"They'll be here in ten minutes," she said after she'd hung up.

"Go!" said Thor to Mandy, but she was already going.

There was a crunch of gears and the van started reversing, the engine whirring, towards where I was hiding.

Ducks took careful aim with the shotgun and blew out the front tire.

The van veered sharply to the right, but kept going.

Ducks took aim again, and blew out the other front tire.

The van came to a stop.

Time for me to make an exit, I thought.

I got back to the scooter, started it up, and was about to take off back down the road when I had a thought.

I delved into my backpack and brought out the plastic bag with the Big Pete's uniform inside.

Taking careful aim, I tossed the bag. Looping through the air, it landed on the roof rack, right next to the wheelchair. I heard a siren, and headlights appeared in the distance, from the direction of Diablo Bay. I got on my scooter, and fifteen minutes later I was just another freeway user.

When I'd planned the escape, my descent from Everest, I'd been reluctant to include Preacher's Forest, but it was too perfect – a buffer zone between rural and urban, the ideal way to introduce myself back onto the city streets.

It had other advantages too.

I took one of the larger paths that led to the lake, stopping close to the edge. The water looked inky, sinister.

Perfect.

I started the scooter up, aimed it towards the lake and ran alongside it until I neared the edge.

Now I was feeling regret: the bike had served me well; it didn't deserve this.

I had no choice, however.

Twisting the throttle, I let go of the handlebars.

The riderless scooter wobbled this way and that before it flew off the edge and smacked into the water.

Inky. Sinister. Perfect.

"These men are springs without water and mists driven by a storm. Blackest darkness is reserved for them!" came a voice.

The Preacher!

Was he responding to what I'd just done, or was this one of his customary nocturnal ravings?

I wasn't going to hang around to find out. I started running. Away from the lake, away from the Preacher, and away from any pursuers. Towards the city with its bright lights still twinkling. *Not for much longer*, I told myself as I checked my watch. *Not for much longer*.

As I left the park, the Preacher's words, "Blackest darkness is reserved for them!" echoed, again and again, in my mind.

DEARTH HOUR

By the time I got off the bus near Taverniti's and walked over to where the Earth Hour people had set up a stage, the adrenaline that had been pumping through my veins had subsided and my heart rate was back to something like normal.

A band was playing – acoustically, of course – to a sparse crowd and people were handing out leaflets explaining climate change. But all around filaments were burning, neon gas was glowing, electricity was flowing – lights were ablaze. Office buildings had floor upon floor checkerboarded with lights. Restaurants shone like beacons, customers, moth-like, fluttering inside. Each cinema was a cathedral of light. And the Manny Hans sign still blazed *MANNY HANS MAKES LIGHTS WORK*.

Earth Hour? It seemed more like Dearth Hour. Dearth of action. Dearth of concern.

Still, when I checked my watch, there was a minute to go.

Don't be so pessimistic, I told myself.

From the stage came the sound of chanting.

Ten. Nine. Eight. Seven. Six. Five. Four. Three. Two. One!

One by one office lights turned off. Some restaurant lights dimmed. Over in Taverniti's I could see the candles burning on each table. A few neon signs flickered before extinguishing. The cinemas seemed less incandescent.

There were cheers from the Earth Hour crowd, but I'd failed.

All that effort, all that planning, and I'd failed.

They must've overridden my override. Or maybe I'd gotten it completely wrong in the first place.

The Manny Hans sign seemed even brighter, more defiant, mocking my failure.

I'd failed and The Debt would come to get me. Come to get my leg. You didn't mess with The Debt. Look at Gus.

The cheering from the Earth Hour crowd suddenly became louder, more raucous. When I looked up, I could see why.

The office buildings were completely dark. Every floor, every office.

So, too, were the cinemas.

The restaurants.

Streetlights.

Only Manny Hans persisted.

But then the sign flickered.

It flickered, and crackled, and expired.

After sixty-seven years, Manny Hans was dead.

A thick, sticky darkness seemed to coat everything. People were cheering. Some were yelling. Others were screaming.

"Daddy, I'm scared," said a kid somewhere. "Hold my hand, Daddy."

I checked my watch – 8:33.

Of course, there'd be a lag; why hadn't I thought of that? Electricity takes time to travel along wires.

I called Imogen.

"I told you I'd do it!" I was about to say, to boast, but I realized that I couldn't.

"I told you it'd happen," I said instead.

"Told me what would happen?" said Imogen.

"That the lights would go out."

"Not here they haven't," she said.

"But in the city all the lights have gone out. It's so freaky."

"Not here they haven't," repeated Imogen.

Immediately I knew what had happened. Halcyon Grove must have its own generator, like essential services such as hospitals have their own generators. And I thought I knew where it was, too.

"Next year I'll do the petition," said Imogen, and I heard the disappointment in her voice. "Next year I'll make them turn off the lights."

Already my mind was racing, already I had yet another plan. But first I had to get back home.

GENERATOR Y

The taxi driver wasn't happy. She reckoned that the hippies responsible for turning off the lights should get the death penalty.

"Electric chair?" I said.

"Hang them by the ruddy neck," said the taxi driver.

By the time we'd reached Halcyon Grove, and I'd paid, it was almost ten past nine.

Imogen was right: the lights were on, and because the rest of the Coast was dark, they seemed brighter, more fluorescent, like the inside of a 7-11 store.

Tristan's sister's bike was where it always was: half on the footpath, half on their front lawn.

Great! Just as I'd hoped.

I looked around: as usual, there was nobody on the streets.

I positioned the bike and stomped hard on the chain with my heel.

It snapped.

"Sorry, Tristan's sister," I mouthed as I picked the chain up and hurried past the tennis courts, towards the anonymous gray building.

It was strange: all those times I'd walked past this building and never known what it was. But now that I was an expert on all things electrical, I figured it must be a backup generator. When the grid went down, this thing kicked in.

The wires looping into the top of the building and the engine hum coming from within confirmed this.

I tried the door. Just as I'd expected: it was locked.

I couldn't stop the generator itself. But there was another way. I stood under the wires, took aim and tossed the bicycle chain. It flew into the air but just missed the wires. Picking it up from the ground, I tried again. This time my aim was better and the chain wrapped around one of the wires, the two ends flailing about.

"Come on!" I yelled. "Come on!"

The chain must've heard me, as one end touched the other wire. It was only a touch, but it was enough to cause a chain reaction, a short circuit. There was a flurry of sparks, then a crack, then the acrid smell of burning. And the lights in Halcyon Grove went out.

I'd won races, I knew what triumph felt like. But that had been nothing compared to what I felt now.

It was like all the electricity I'd denied was now zinging through me. I was glowing. I was luminescent. I was incandescent.

But then I remembered Tristan's email: *c u there when its dark!*

And all the light went out of me.

Ω Ω Ω

Like all the other houses in Halcyon Grove, Imogen's had been swallowed by the darkness, but unlike the other houses there weren't flashes of light, excited talk, as residents, armed with flashlights, attempted to do something about it. No, her house was very dark and very quiet, just a bit spooky. And there was no response when I knocked on the door.

"It's me, Dom," I yelled through the keyhole.

"Dom?" came a faint voice from the other side of the door.

"Yes, Mrs. Havilland, it's me!" I said.

A click, as the door unlocked. I pushed it open.

Mrs. Havilland was wearing a dressing gown and fluffy slippers, and was holding a candle that threw a flickering light over her puffy white face.

"What's happening?" she said. "Why have the televisions stopped working?"

"It's a blackout, Mrs. Havilland," I said, looking at my watch. "The power will come back on in thirteen minutes."

Well, I hoped the power would come back on in thirteen minutes.

"Where's Imogen?" I asked.

"I don't know," said Mrs. Havilland.

"You don't know?"

"I mean, she was here, but then the lights went out and I couldn't find her anymore. She's okay, isn't she?"

"I'm sure she's fine," I said. "Did you try calling her?"

"She doesn't answer."

I took out my phone and tried her number. It rang, but she didn't answer.

"You don't think something's happened to her, do you?" said Mrs. Havilland, her voice becoming increasingly fretful.

"I'm sure she's fine," I said.

And I was sure she was fine, she was just with Tristan, that was all.

And that was her choice, I told myself.

But she didn't know Tristan like I knew Tristan. To him she was just a conquest, a notch on his belt, somebody he could brag about to his mates. And I couldn't let her become that. Not Imogen. I moved closer to Mrs. Havilland, and as I did I smelled the alcohol, the fumes crawling up my nostrils.

"So do you want me to go and find her?" I asked her.

"Please," she said.

"So when she asks, you can tell her that you asked me to find her?"

"Yes, of course," she said.

"Okay," I said. "I'm going to do what you asked me to do. Don't worry, Mrs. Havilland, the lights will be back on soon."

There was a lot of noise coming from inside the Jazys' house. At first I thought they were really freaking out and I felt a bit guilty – obviously not everybody enjoys a blackout. But as I got closer I could hear people making spooky noises followed by screams of laughter.

I went to step off the footpath and onto the Jazys' lawn, but something made me hesitate. It didn't take me long to realize what it was. So far, all the crazy stuff I'd done tonight had been for one reason and one reason only: The Debt. Really, I'd had no choice: either I did it, or they took my leg. Like I said, no choice. But this had nothing at all to do with The Debt. With this, I did have a choice.

I hesitated, but then I crossed the line, stepping off the footpath and onto the grass.

And as I did I had this feeling that I'd left something behind.

Something intangible but irretrievable.

I kept going, remembering how Alpha and Thor had moved, how they'd seemed to glide across the ground.

I stopped by the bay window, trying to work out if any of the spooky noises, any of the laughter, belonged to Imogen, but they didn't, so I kept going, ninja-ing along the side of the house.

At the back of the house an expanse of lawn, host to an array of rattan furniture, led to an enormous blue-tiled pool.

Okay, maybe it wasn't quite as enormous as our pool, but it was a fair size.

On the other side of the pool was another, separate building. It was dark on the outside, dark on the inside.

I'd heard Tristan bragging about his "man cave" before, telling everybody how private it was, how he could do anything he liked in there.

That had to be it.

Was she in there?

I took out my phone, called her number. Inside the man cave, a Lady Gaga song played.

I wanted to go and bash on the glass sliding doors.

"Imogen," I wanted to say. "You have to come out, now."

But I knew, if I did that, Imogen would know I'd been monitoring her emails. How else would I know exactly where she was right now?

And if she knew that, then she would hate me forever. And I wouldn't blame her. I had to find another way to get her out of there.

But how?

And again I had the feeling that I had a choice here. That I could walk away right now.

But again, I kept going.

I crept along the side of Tristan's pad, across a further expanse of lawn, until I came to a shed. The door was unlocked, so I pushed it open. Using my iPhone flashlight app, I checked out what was inside.

There was an enormous riding mower; a battery of whipper-snippers; an arsenal of gleaming gardening equipment.

But it was the humble can of fuel that caught my arsonist's eyes.

I grabbed it, and some matches, and ninja-ed back to the pool.

I unscrewed the cap, and was about to slosh the contents into the water, when I hesitated.

Was there any chance of the house catching fire, too?

No, it was too far away.

Satisfied that I wasn't about to barbecue the entire Jazy clan, I upended the can's contents into the pool.

But then I thought of all those cop shows I'd seen on TV: my fingerprints would be all over the can now.

Whatever, I thought, as I tossed the can into the water.

I waited until the fuel had dispersed across the pool's surface before, standing well back, I took out a match, lit it and flicked it towards the pool.

The match extinguished before it hit the surface.

I tried again, and this time it worked. Really worked. *Whoosh!* Two-meter-high flames danced across the surface; dirty smoke billowed upwards.

As far as destroying forensic evidence went, tossing the can in the pool had been an excellent idea. As far as occupational health and safety went, perhaps not so excellent.

Because just as I stepped back behind a hydrangea bush, there was an explosion, the second major *kaboom!* of the night. And an almighty spout of water gushed into the air.

By some strange optical trick, I could make out my reflection in it. I was grinning, a contorted grin, like a demented gargoyle. Then the spout dispersed and my image was eaten up by the flames.

The sliding doors to Tristan's studio slid open, and Tristan appeared. Guns blazing, six pack six-packing; he wasn't wearing a shirt. Shorts but no shirt.

Right then, I wanted another bomb, one to blow him and his six pack to kingdom come.

Imogen appeared after him.

She was, thankfully, fully dressed. Disheveled, but fully dressed.

Pfft! More noises.

I looked behind me – the rattan furniture was catching fire, a daisy chain of firebombs, taking the flames inevitably towards the house.

Tristan's little sister was the first to appear at the back door, followed by her parents.

I ran to the garden hose, wrenched the tap to full. The pressure was good and I was able to quickly douse the rattan-fueled flames.

Then there was a lull, everybody just standing there, shocked, staring at the half-empty pool, not knowing what to say.

Eventually Tristan's little sister said, "The poor Kreepy Krauly."

I could see what she meant: the blackened carcass of the award-winning pool cleaner was floating on the surface.

"Almost poor us," said Mr. Jazy, looking at me, smiling.

"What the blazes were you doing here?" said Tristan.

The pun, I'm sure, was unintentional.

"I could hear the explosion from up the street," I said. "So I came running."

"Lucky he did," said Mr. Jazy.

But Tristan was having none of it. "That quickly?" he said.

More people were arriving now, most of them neighbors. But among them was Roberto, strangely out of context with all those home owners.

"I saw some kids running off," he said loudly. "Looked like street kids from Surfers."

"They'll be on CCTV then," said somebody else.

"Power's down," said somebody else. "There is no CCTV."

And then everybody was talking and there was no mistaking the collective sense of unease, of shock.

I couldn't blame them, I'd had the same feelings not so long ago when the walls had been breached; Halcyon Grove was no longer quite so halcyon.

I was ready to make my retreat when I noticed that Tristan was holding Imogen's hand.

Holding it!

243

Retreat, my rectum.

I moved closer to Imogen and said, "Your mum's been looking for you."

"You saw her?" she said.

"Yeah, she got scared in that dark house all by herself."

Imogen let go of Tristan's hand.

"I can walk back with you if you like," I said.

"Thanks," said Imogen.

We'd just reached Imogen's house when the lights went back on. I checked my watch: 9:33.

THE STATE TITLES

Everybody wanted to go to the race, even Toby.

"Just love to watch my big bro perform," he said.

But as we were all waiting for Dad outside our house I heard him say to Mom, "Laziko's is on the way, isn't it?"

Now I understood why Toby wanted to go to the race: Laziko's had the best kebabs on the Coast.

But what about me? Did I want to go to the race?

If you'd asked me that during the last few days, my answer would've been an emphatic "no."

Compared to The Debt, running around and around in a circle seemed so trivial, almost silly.

Especially not on Monday, after Dad had added an *A* brand to the *P* brand and the inside of my thigh had burned all night.

But today when I woke up I realized I'd changed my mind.

The Debt wasn't going to stop me from doing what I loved most in the world. I just wasn't going to let them.

A minibus pulled up, jerking to a stop, Dad driving, Dad smiling.

Because he got driven everywhere by Marcus, Dad didn't drive much, so when he did he got a little bit excited.

"This bad boy's got some grunt," he said as we took our seats.

"Bad boy?" said Gus.

"Yeah, get with it, Pops," said Dad. "It's all about bad boys these days, isn't it, kids?"

Miranda and Toby agreed: "Yes, Dad, it's all about bad boys."

But I wasn't so sure. About bad boys. Or about my dad, my Calabrian-speaking dad.

While I'd been busy with The Debt, I hadn't been able to give much thought to what I'd witnessed at Nimbin. But now that I'd actually managed to make good the repayment it was constantly on my mind. When I looked at my dad, smiling his goofy smile, he hadn't changed a bit. But when I thought of him speaking Calabrian, he had changed. How could he not?

The radio was tuned to Classic Rock FM, and "(I Can't Get No) Satisfaction" by The Rolling Stones was playing.

"And listen to this bad boy," Dad said, turning up the volume.

Even more "(I Can't Get No) Satisfaction" by The Rolling Stones.

We pulled up outside Imogen's house.

She was waiting for us, wearing a flowery dress, wearing high heels, like she was going to the theatre, not a race, but I suppose when you go out as infrequently as Imogen, you're going to make the most of it.

I could see Mrs. Havilland standing at the upstairs window, waving good-bye. From the forlorn look on her face, even paler than usual, you would think that her daughter was going away for months, perhaps even years, not just a few hours.

"Poor Beth," said Mom to Dad. "She really is getting worse."

"Poor Beth," repeated Dad.

How would you say that in Calabrian, Dad? I thought.

"This is so cool," said Imogen as she sat down next to me.

I could see, however, that Gus was thinking it wasn't cool at all, that he was thinking this was

247

not how a serious athlete prepared for a race. He'd wanted to drive up with just the two of us in his old truck, but Mom had insisted that we all go together, that we go "as a family."

Gus needn't have worried, though, because I felt great. Better than great. What were a few laps of the track for somebody who'd turned off – and turned back on – the city's lights?

It was an hour's drive to the venue, over the hinterland, towards where the sun was now setting. This bad boy may have had some grunt, but Dad wasn't utilizing much of it. He drove very slowly, cautiously negotiating the many turns.

"I can take over if you like, darling," suggested Mom, but Dad was having none of it.

"I've got it," he said.

On the radio they were talking about the blackout. Because of the timing – from eight thirty-three to nine thirty-three – initial suspicion had fallen on the Earth Hour organization. An investigative journalist by the name of Phil Cher was confident that any enquiry would clear them of all responsibility, however. Instead, he was pointing the finger at the Diablo Bay Power Station. Initially they'd denied any responsibility, but now they were conducting "an exhaustive internal investigation" as to whether there had been an "unforeseen technical glitch." Somebody else from an organization called The Campaign Against Nuclear Energy said that this showed how vulnerable the station was and it should be now "shut down permanently."

"I bet you some black hat hacked into their network," said Miranda.

"Somebody from Earth Hour?" I said.

"No, not them, they're too goody-goody," said Miranda, looking straight at me. "I reckon it was a lone wolf."

Now they were talking about the fire in Halcyon Grove, wondering if the two were connected, whether the pool had been lit as a sort of diversionary tactic.

"What are you smiling at?" Imogen said to me.

"Smiling? Me?"

"Smiling. You."

"I was thinking of something else," I said, the mother of all lies.

"Blazing bells and buckets of blood!" said Gus. "Can you turn that thing off? Dom needs some quiet before the race."

Dad switched off the radio and I got my quiet before the race.

It was dark when we arrived, but the stadium was all lit up. I was surprised at all the cars in the parking lot, all the people walking about. Track running wasn't exactly the most popular spectator sport in this country. Not like in Finland or Sweden, where they'll get a crowd of a hundred thousand just to see twelve athletes run four laps.

"There's a gozleme stall!" said Toby, whose love of a Laziko's kebab was only matched by his love of a Turkish savory pastry.

"This is so cool!" said Imogen.

Anybody would think we'd just arrived at Disneyland, not some running track.

Despite Dad's tortuous driving, we were early, so I had twenty minutes before I was due to meet the rest of the team. Gus and I found a quiet place and discussed tactics. He wanted me to race conservatively, stay in the pack but keep in touch with the leaders, and kick with two hundred meters to go.

"Sure it'd be a nice race to win," he said, "but it's more important that you qualify for the national titles, that you finish in the first six."

Nothing radical there: sit-and-kick was my usual tactic. In fact, it was the usual tactic of most middle-distance runners.

Front-running was for fools, Gus always said, for people like Rashid who seemed to have a psychological need to get in the lead. Front-runners used too much energy. Front-runners never won.

Gus never talked about the 1974 Commonwealth

Games, however, where the great Tanzanian runner Filbert Bayi led from the front to win gold and break the world 1500-meter record. And I was sick of sitting in packs, among all the wayward spikes, all the pointy elbows, in that moving cocoon of BO.

Gus could go on about front-running fools as much as he liked, because I'd already made up my mind. I'd turned off the city's lights; today I was going to do a Filbert Bayi; today I was going to put daylight between me and the pack from start to finish.

"Sure," I said to Gus. "Stay in the pack, keep in touch with the leaders, kick with two hundred to go."

"That's the ticket," he said.

Coach Sheeds and Gus didn't agree on many things, but they agreed about this: I was a sit-and-kick sort of runner.

"Stay in the pack, keep in touch with the leaders," Coach Sheeds told me in the locker room. "And –"

"I know, I know," I said impatiently. "Kick with two hundred meters to go."

Outside, as Rashid, Charles, Gabby and I did our warm-up exercises on the side of the track, the four Kenyans from Brisbane Boys appeared. There was a sort of collective gasp from the other runners. I had to admit, with their lithe, lean physiques, their skin black and glossy under the lights, their loose, confident way of walking, they did look a bit intimidating.

But when Rashid whispered, "We're doomed," to me, I wanted to say to him: *They're only Kenyans. Made from the same stuff that you and I are made from: muscle, sinew, blood.*

We breathe the same air.

Eat the same food (well, I do, anyway).

And tell me, Rashid, has one of those Kenyans you are so in awe of ever blown up a swimming pool?

No, I didn't think so.

Bring it on, Kenyans.

"Get ready," said the starter, and I took my position on the line, crouching slightly.

The gun went off and so did we.

Cheers from the crowd as I jostled past Rashid.

"Dom, what's happening?" he said, but I didn't have time to answer.

I took the lead, almost sprinting the first lap.

"Go, Dom!" I could hear Imogen yell as I passed.

I glanced behind. The Kenyans were twenty or so meters back, a wave of them, a wall of them. I glanced at the clock: 59.16 seconds. I was on track for a sub four-minute race, an Australian record for a fifteen year old. And why not – I'd turned off the city's lights.

Out of the corner of my eye I could see Coach Sheeds gesturing frantically with her hands – *slow down, slow down, slow down!*

I heard Gus's voice. "Dom, hand brake on!"

But I didn't slow down. I didn't put the hand brake on.

It was 1974. It was the Commonwealth Games. And I was Filbert Bayi.

It was starting to hurt now, but I maintained the pace.

As I completed the second lap and moved into the third I again looked behind.

The Kenyans were even further back.

Again I checked the clock. One minute fifty-eight seconds.

I was still on record pace.

"Go, Dom!" yelled Dad.

"Go, Dom! yelled Mom.

"Go, Dom!" yelled Miranda.

"Go, Dom!" yelled Toby.

Toby?

I'd almost finished the third lap when it happened, when I hit a wall so big that, like the Great Wall of China, it would surely have been visible from outer space.

The track was now treacle and I could hardly lift my legs out of it.

The Kenyans swarmed past me.

Gus's words came back to me: *front-runners are fools*.

"Come on, Dom!" urged Rashid as he ran alongside me. "There's only three hundred to go."

Three hundred? It may as well have been three thousand, three million.

I glanced behind: the pack was closing in.

Looked ahead: the Kenyans were kicking, racing down the home straight.

This time, nobody was going to save me.

"Go!" I said to Rashid.

He surged, leaving me behind. Then Charles passed me.

At least they'd go to the nationals, I thought, as I watched the Kenyans make for the finish line.

And then every light in the stadium went out.

SKIN ON SKIN

Mom was driving, and she hammered the hairpin turns, working the gears like a Formula One driver.

"They'll have to run the race again," Gus explained to Dad.

"Maybe this time Dom might actually keep running," said Toby, looking over at me.

"I did keep running, you tub of lard," I said, reaching across to thump him on the arm.

"Dom!" said Mom.

Although it was dark inside the bus, I knew that Gus was giving me a look that said he was with Toby on this: maybe I hadn't actually stopped running, but I'd run a really, really dumb race.

And I couldn't argue with him. The dumbest race I'd run in my running life.

"I wonder if it was the same hacker who turned the lights off during Earth Hour?" said Miranda.

I had a ready answer to her question – no, it wasn't, Miranda – but I couldn't very well give it to her.

But I did wonder something: I'd turned the lights off for The Debt. Had they returned the favor and turned the lights off for me?

"What is this idiot behind us doing?" said Mom.

I looked back.

We were being tailgated by a white van, streamlined, sort of futuristic-looking.

As we came out of another hairpin, the van moved out as if to pass.

"What is he doing?" Mom said.

I could see what she meant: there was no clear road ahead; it was a suicidal place to pass.

The van was alongside us, a shadowed face appearing at the passenger window.

Mom stepped on the brakes, giving the van the space to move in front of us.

As she did, light washed over the van, and the face, for a split second, was visible.

Seb!

No, it couldn't be.

A truck was coming the other way, lights flashing, horn blaring.

Just when it seemed a crash was inevitable, the van spurted ahead of us and the truck passed.

"What an idiot!" said Mom as its taillights disappeared around another bend.

But Dad, strangely, said nothing.

We came down off the range and onto the flatland of the coast, the vegetal smell of the hinterland becoming the clean salt smell of the ocean.

In the dark, Imogen's hand found my hand. Her shoulder leaned against my shoulder. Her face turned towards my face.

The Debt, my father speaking in tongues, the race I'd just run, all the stuff of the last few weeks faded into the background and all that was left was this feeling, her skin on my skin, my breath mingling with her breath.

And Imogen, who had been quiet for the whole trip, whispered, "Hey, Dom, I didn't want to bother you before the race, but can I ask you a question?"

"Sure," I said.

"Did you set fire to the Jazys' pool?"

I had plenty of reasons to lie, but one really good reason not to: Imogen was the best friend I'd ever had.

"Yes, I did," I whispered.

"Why?"

"Because I didn't want you in there with Tristan."

It probably took only ten seconds, but it felt like an eternity, an eternity during which I realized how important Imogen was to me, how devastated I would be if my setting fire to the Jazys' pool somehow ended our friendship.

And then Imogen's skin was no longer on my skin, her breath no longer mingled with my breath.

"Imogen?" I whispered, but she had already turned away from me.

'FESS UP

Mr. Travers was one of those teachers with a voice that seemed to suck all the oxygen out of the classroom. As all athletes – and many non-athletes – know, the body needs oxygen, and plenty of it, in order to function properly. Without sufficient oxygen, the body shuts down. So you're not exactly asleep, but you're not exactly awake either. You're in in-between land, zombie land, wishing that something would happen, anything, to interrupt Mr. Travers's incessant oxygen-depleting drone.

But when it did happen, when there was a knock on the door, when this kid in a neck brace handed Mr. Travers an official-looking piece of paper, I wondered if I'd done too much wishing. And when Mr. Travers studied the paper and said, "Dominic Silvagni is to report to the office immediately," I knew I'd done too much wishing.

Now everybody was awake, alert, and the whispering started.

"What could Silvagni have done?"

"But Silvagni never gets in trouble."

As I walked past Tristan's empty desk, I imagined him giving me a playful punch on the arm. Playful for him, painful for me.

I imagined him saying, "You're so busted."

And immediately I thought of those mad flames dancing across the surface of his swimming pool and wondered if they'd finally worked out who did it, whether this imagined Tristan was right and I was "so busted."

Weirdly enough, though, I was also pleased that I'd managed to get out of the classroom, managed to escape the drone. But when I got to the principal's office and he told me, in that precise, over-enunciated voice of his, that some detectives – de-tec-tives – were here to have a chat about the recent excursion – ex-cur-sion – to the Diablo Bay Nuclear Power Station, the excitement evaporated pretty quickly.

"Unfortunately I have a meeting and can't be there," he said. "But Mr. Ryan will be present."

When I found myself sitting at a table, my civics teacher on one side of me, while two detectives, one male, one female, sat on the other side and battered me with question after question, I knew I was far, far better off in in-between land.

"But you have your culprits, don't you?" said Mr. Ryan. "It was in the paper – three members of some radical eco-group."

"Yes, they are definitely in the frame," said the female detective.

"In the frame?" said Mr. Ryan. "From what I read they're in jail!"

The male detective gave a sort of half shrug like it hadn't been his idea to incarcerate them.

As for his colleague, she didn't seem the least bit concerned whether they had the culprits or not.

"So let me get this straight – this whole excursion was your idea?" she asked.

She'd been very friendly, very smiley, but I was pretty sure that friendly and smiley were not the reasons somebody got awarded a detective's badge.

My guts, which had been churning, churned some more. And my palms, which had been sweating, sweated some more.

I really didn't want to say a thing, because it seemed that anything that came out of my mouth would be incriminating, but when I looked over at Mr. Ryan he gave me an encouraging nod.

So I let some words come out of my mouth, two of them: "That's right."

The detectives exchanged looks and I thought that was it – only two words, but enough to get me locked up forever.

More churning.

More sweating.

But why was Mr. Ryan smiling confidently at me, and then at the detectives? Like he was almost enjoying this? Let's face it, he was my civics teacher, not some hotshot lawyer from some legal show. I half expected him to say, "My client refuses to answer any more questions," just like they did on TV, but instead he said, "Dominic came to me with his idea for the excursion and I saw it as an excellent learning opportunity for my students."

The male detective, who had also been friendly and smiley, though not quite as much as his colleague, consulted a piece of paper before he said, "And this whole shebang was paid for by Dominic's father?"

"That's absolutely correct," said Mr. Ryan.

"That's a bit unusual, isn't it?" said the detective.

"No, not at all. We're a private school, and as such rely heavily on the largesse of our parent body."

The detectives exchanged looks, and I wondered if they weren't sure what "largesse" meant either.

"Will that be all now?" said Mr. Ryan. "Both Dominic and I have classes to get to."

Mr. Ryan might have only been a civics teacher, but he was doing an excellent job of impersonating a hotshot lawyer from some legal show.

The female detective took something from the folder, and placed it on the table.

It was a grainy photo. A still obviously lifted from CCTV footage. Somebody in a Big Pete's Pizzas uniform. Wearing a helmet.

"Do either of you know who this is?" she asked.

I looked across at her, at her eyes flicking between me and the photo. And I was sure she knew that they were the same person.

And now my whole body was churning, and my whole body was sweating.

The game was up.

Might as well 'fess up.

And, suddenly, I felt this immense sense of impending relief, because at last I could tell somebody the whole crazy story.

The story that started on the day I turned fifteen.

The female detective repeated her question. "Do either of you know who this is?"

The words, "It's me" were on the tip of my tongue, ready to make their way into the world.

Good-bye freedom. Good-bye leg. If the cops didn't get me, then The Debt surely would.

"Look, this is ridiculous," said Mr. Ryan. "We've allowed you to talk to our student, but this is becoming something else. This is harassment."

The detectives exchanged looks, and then they gathered their papers.

"Dom, we'll see you later," said the male detective.

The female detective looked me straight in the eyes and said, "We *will* see you later."

They thanked us for our time and exited the room.

I recalled what she'd said – *We* will *see you later* – and it sent a shiver right through my body.

The good guys weren't even on my side, now.

But then I realized that Mr. Ryan was still there with me.

"Wow," I said. "You were just like a lawyer, Mr. Ryan."

"Dom," said Mr. Ryan, "I am a lawyer."

As we walked back he explained it to me. He'd been a barrister, down in Sydney, but the job hadn't given him the satisfaction he'd thought it would. So he'd retrained as a teacher and come back to teach at the same school that he'd attended. Where he still held one of the cross-country running records.

"That's great," I said, though I wasn't sure if I believed it. Why would anybody become a teacher, especially a lawyer? Still, I was incredibly glad he'd been in there with me.

When we reached the classroom I excused myself and went to the bathroom.

There were five other kids in there, doing what I was about to do: checking their phones.

When I turned mine on, there was a flurry of beeps. I had fifty-seven new messages! As I scrolled through them it became clear that actually I had the same message fifty-seven times.

It said: *discipule, caro mortua es.*

INSTALLMENT ONE

THE DEBT

PHILLIP GWYNNE

CATCH THE ZOLT

LESSON ONE: DON'T MESS WITH THE DEBT

INSTALLMENT TWO

THE DEBT

PHILLIP GWYNNE

TURN OFF THE LIGHTS

INSTALLMENT THREE

THE DEBT

PHILLIP GWYNNE

BRING BACK CERBERUS

LESSON THREE: YOU NEVER KNOW WHO'S LISTENING

INSTALLMENT FOUR

THE DEBT

PHILLIP GWYNNE

FETCH THE TREASURE HUNTER

LESSON FOUR: SOME HACKS CAN'T BE WON

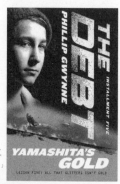

INSTALLMENT FIVE

THE DEBT

PHILLIP GWYNNE

YAMASHITA'S GOLD

LESSON FIVE: ALL THAT GLITTERS ISN'T GOLD

INSTALLMENT SIX

THE DEBT

PHILLIP GWYNNE

TAKE A LIFE

LESSON SIX: HE THAT DIES, PAYS ALL DEBTS